Blaeberry Sunday

Elizabeth O'Hara

PRAISE FOR *BLAEBERRY SUNDAY*

"The bittersweet mood of the story is wonderfully
encapsulated in the events of Blaeberry Sunday itself . . ."

PRAISE FOR *THE HIRING FAIR*

"A moving story with a memorable heroine at its heart."
Sunday Independent

"A lovely read . . . "
The Irish Times

POOLBEG

For Doireann and Clara

Published in 1994 by
Poolbeg,
A division of Poolbeg Enterprises Ltd,
Knocksedan House,
123 Baldoyle Industrial Estate
Dublin 13, Ireland

© Elizabeth O'Hara 1994

Reprinted May 1995
Reprinted June 1995

The moral right of the author has been asserted.

The Publishers gratefully acknowledge the assistance of The Arts Council.

A catalogue record for this book is available from the British Library.

ISBN 1 85371 360 0

Cover painting by Tom Roche
Cover design by Poolbeg Group Services Ltd
Set by Poolbeg Group Services Ltd in Garamond 10/13.5
Printed by The Guernsey Press Co Ltd,
Vale, Guernsey, Channel Islands.

CONTENTS

A NOTE ON THE AUTHOR

Elizabeth O'Hara is the pseudonym of Eilís Ni Dhuibhne, a well-known novelist and short story writer. Her books for children include *The Uncommon Cormorant, Hugo and the Sunshine Girl* and *The Hiring Fair*.

1

Sally Comes Home

"So many flies!" Katie complained, dodging a fuzzy cloud of midges. "They're eating me alive!"

"So many flowers!" said Sally, sticking her nose into a clump of meadow-sweet and taking it out again quickly; meadow-sweet does not really smell all that nice. "So many bees! Such a clear blue sky!"

"It's too hot, no matter what you say." Katie gave her sister a friendly kick. "And I'm tired. I wish we were home."

"We will be in five minutes," said Sally, swatting one of the flies which had taken a fancy to her eyelid. "No point in getting impatient now!"

Summer 1893. The warmest summer anyone in the north west of Ireland had ever experienced. It was only May but already there was real heat in the sun. Sally and Katie were on their way home from Tyrone to Donegal where they had spent their second winter working as hired girls with the Stewarts and Campbells of Ballygowl. To avoid having to carry them, they both wore their heaviest clothes – all of them. Sally, a tall dark-haired girl, wore a red petticoat. Over that she had a drugget skirt, striped red and green, and over that another skirt of dark blue wool. Completing the outfit were a white blouse, red vest and brown jacket. She carried her thick black shawl on her arm. Across her shoulder was a stick with a cotton bundle tied to the end of it. The bundle contained all her belongings, apart, that is, from those which she was already wearing. Katie, who was smaller than her sister and fair-haired, had a petticoat, a cotton dress, a long rust-coloured tweed skirt, and a black jacket. She too carried a woollen shawl and shouldered a bundle. Both girls wore stockings and winter boots on their feet, and straw hats on their heads. They looked a bit like overdressed scarecrows. That they felt hot was not surprising.

They had started the journey from Ballygowl at six o'clock yesterday morning. First they travelled by train to Strabane, which was as far as the railway went. They spent the night in the house of a cousin of their mother's, Maggie Doherty. Then they took a ride on a horse and cart to Letterkenny. Finally they got a lift from two fishermen who were coming from the fish market in Letterkenny to a hamlet just two miles from Glenbra. That part of the journey, in a light coracle, was the best. A cool breeze blew across the lough and fanned the girls' sunburned faces. Sally slouched on a sack in the stern of the boat, screwing up her eyes so she could see the millions of silver swords glinting on the water, opening them again to stare at the terns dropping like stones into the waves. She breathed deeply, savouring the tang of salt and fish. She had not forgotten what the landscape close to her home was like, but she had not thought about it for some time. Only now did she realise how much she had missed home: not just her house and her mother and family, but the sights and the sounds, the sea and even the air. It was like seeing a good friend you have almost forgotten about, but as soon as you see them you realise how much you like everything about them, the way they look and the way they sound, the things they say. It felt wonderful.

Arriving at the house, however, was not a moment of unmixed pleasure. It was not that home itself did not look attractive: the sun was still shining when Katie and Sally turned the corner into the yard. The sycamore trees were at their best, lightly covered in pale green foliage like girls in new summer dresses. The chickens clucked and pecked among the mossy cobbles and the stone wall that surrounded the yard was bordered by thousands of late primroses. The house itself looked just as friendly as always, its red door like a rosy mouth, its two windows like two eyes winking at you inviting you to share a joke.

Sally did not know why she felt uneasy as she walked up to the door; she had been given to sudden swings of mood lately. She could be perfectly happy at one minute, as she had been in the boat, and then a few minutes later feel anxious and miserable for some very minor reason. Maybe she was disappointed because her mother and sister Janey were not out in the yard to meet them. That didn't make sense, though. There was no way they could have known exactly when Sally and Katie would arrive. They did not even know exactly which day it would be. All they knew, from the letter Sally had sent them about a fortnight ago, was that they would be leaving Ballygowl early in May, and making their way back to Donegal. They wouldn't even be thinking of exact dates. Early May. They would just hope sooner rather than later, but they would never have been able to guess just when.

Sally and Katie pushed open the half-door and went

into the kitchen. The fire was burning low on the hearth, the black kettle swinging on the crane to one side of it. Someone had put a posy of wild bluebells in a jam jar on the windowsill. The dresser stood in its place against the back wall, decked with flowery tea-bowls and yellow basins.

But nobody was at home.

Sally and Katie looked at each other in dismay.

"They must be out somewhere," said Sally, tossing her bundle onto the floor and pulling off her jacket. She felt like crying. Katie placed her bundle carefully on a straw-seated chair. Sally started to look around the house, into the "room" and the bedrooms at the other side of it. Katie stayed in the kitchen, taking off some of her clothes and tidying up her hair.

Suddenly a voice said: "I want a light for my pipe."

"Oh God!" said Sally, who was back in the kitchen. She'd discarded two of her skirts by now, as well as her footwear. She was dressed only in her petticoat and blouse and feeling very comfortable. "Granny!"

She went over to the curtained-off bed in a recess next to the fire and looked inside. Granny was lying against her pillow, her white hair untidily straggling against her yellowish cheeks. Her eyes were half closed.

"Hello Granny," she said. "How are you?"

"Terrible," said Granny. "I am dying and nobody gives a tinker's curse. They won't give me enough tobacco, they are so niggardly, the devil take the lot of them!"

"We're home, Granny," Sally said, leaning over and giving the old woman a kiss on the forehead. "Katie and I have come home."

"Get me a light from the fire," said Granny, opening her eyes and peering at Sally. Her eyes were very big and very blue, but there was a white film over the pupils. Her sight was very bad and in the dark kitchen she could hardly see anything.

Sally lit a bit of brushwood and brought it over to the bed. Granny took it in her shaking hands and after a while managed to get her pipe lit. She dragged deeply on it, and then lay back against her pillow, looking much happier.

"Do you know where Mother and Janey are, Granny?"

Granny did not answer. She smoked her pipe a bit more.

"We've come home," Sally was not going to give up easily. "Katie and I, we've been in Tyrone, working as hired girls. But now we're home and we are going to stay here for the whole summer. At least I am. We travelled all day yesterday and most of today. It was a very long journey."

"I went to Scotland when I was a girl," said Granny, suddenly deciding to take part in this conversation. "I went tatie hoking with Paddy Greene's gang."

"That must have been nice, Granny," said Sally.

"It was terrible," said Granny. "I hated every minute of it. Scotland is a desperate place. I had to work for sixteen hours a day and sleep in a barn. There was never enough to eat. We got rotten potatoes and sour milk, that was all."

"Oh dear. Did you do that more than once?"

"The barn burnt down in the end." Granny was not listening again. "I heard that later. It burnt down. Fifteen people were burned to death. Molly Lynch was burned. She was my best friend. Nineteen years of age. Burned to a cinder. That's how it was. MacDonald's barn. I wasn't there then. I was married. I came home and married Turlough Gallagher. I didn't have to go tatie hoking after that. He had two cows. So I wasn't in the barn. That's how it was."

Granny puffed at her pipe.

Sally and Katie were quiet for a moment. Sally wished Granny hadn't told that story. She'd heard it before, more than once, but it seemed particularly discouraging just now.

"We were lucky, in Tyrone," she said, after a while. "It wasn't so bad, they were good to us. Do you know where Mother and Janey are, Granny?"

Granny had stopped talking.

"She probably doesn't know anyway," said Katie, sensibly. "Why don't we just unpack and wait? They'll be back soon enough. Will we have something to eat?"

"I'm hungry," said Sally. "But I'd rather wait for them, wouldn't you? Why don't we have some milk while we're waiting? That'll keep the edge off our hunger."

Mrs Gallagher, their mother, and Janey, came in just as they were finishing their bowls of milk.

"Mother of God!" said Mrs Gallagher, "I don't believe it."

"Here we are!" said Sally, giving her a hug. She made her voice sound as cheerful as possible. But the odd thing was that, although she had been crying a few minutes ago because her mother was not at home, seeing her made her feel uneasy, too. She withdrew quickly from the hug.

Katie kissed her mother on the cheek and picked up Janey and gave her a swing.

"Oh Janey!" said Sally. "You look gorgeous! You are beautiful!"

"Oh now, handsome is as handsome does," said Mrs Gallagher, tightening her mouth. It worried her when people praised her children's looks: it was thought that such praise was unlucky. If the fairies heard it they would be tempted to steal the child who was thought to be beautiful.

"Are you a good girl?" Katie was asking Janey. It was all right to be good. The fairies were not interested in good children!

Janey stood in complete silence, fluttering her eyelashes. She glanced at the red bundle on the table from time to time: she'd caught sight of that as soon as she walked in the door.

"Don't worry, we've got some sweeties for you all right. We wouldn't forget them would we?"

Janey smiled tentatively, as if she had doubts about that.

"But first you're going to tell us what you have been doing since we saw you last. Then you get the sweeties. All right?"

Janey nodded but her eyes lost some of their shine. Sally tossed her head. She did not see the point of making Janey wait. The sweets were in the bundles, they were for her. Why did Katie have to play these games, making the little girl wait?

Suddenly everything seemed wrong to Sally.

"You've been helping Mammy in the house, haven't you?"

Janey nodded.

"And you've been playing with Mary Ann?"

Janey nodded again.

"Have you started going to school?"

Janey nodded and then shook her head mischievously.

"There," said Sally. "Now you've told us everything that has happened. And here," she said, going to her bundle and opening it, "is your present!"

She handed Janey a brown paper bag. Janey sat down on the floor and opened it. A heap of sweets tumbled out onto the floor. There were three big lumps of brown rock, three sugar sticks, striped pink and green, and no less than a dozen black and white bull's-eyes. She fingered them lovingly, counted them, picked them up and looked at them: she had never had so many sweets. It was like being in heaven.

"Aren't you going to eat some?" asked Sally.

Janey smiled up at her. She loved the look of the sweets so much that she didn't want to start eating them. She knew enough about herself to realise that once she started she wouldn't want to stop, and then all the delicious sweets would be gone. She continued to play with them and didn't put even one in her mouth for the time being.

"I've got something else as well," said Katie. "Would you like to have it now or later?"

"Now," said Janey without a moment's hesitation.

"All right. Put the sweets back in the bag for a minute, and I'll give it to you."

Mrs Gallagher was looking on, smiling. Sally wondered what Katie had got. She hadn't told her about it. Even Granny had stuck her head out through the curtains of her bed and was trying to get a good view of what was going on.

Katie took an oblong paper parcel out of her bundle: it was surprising how much that little cloth bundle could hold. The parcel was tied up with hairy string, and Janey had difficulty in getting it untied. She managed, however. Inside the first layer of paper was another layer. She pulled it off impatiently, and the two sheets went fluttering to the floor.

Then she had to remove a few layers of soft white tissue. She pulled at this more carefully, since it had a lovely mysterious quality to it: she hadn't felt that sort of paper before. Slowly it peeled away.

"Dolly!" Janey breathed softly.

"Dolly!"

Her eyes shone like stars and her face was one huge smile of wonder and delight. Lying in a bed of white tissue was the most beautiful doll she had ever seen. It had a round white face, with red lips and blue eyes, and fair curling hair, quite like Janey's own baby hair. It was dressed in a frock of white muslin sprigged with green. On its hands were white gloves, real kid, and it had a white lace cap on its head.

"Goodness, Katie," said Sally, who had never seen such a doll either. Even the Stewart children didn't have toys like that. "Where did you get that?"

"Old Mrs Campbell," said Katie. "She has a trunk of old stuff up in the gallery. Suddenly, the day before I left, when I was telling her about Janey and that, she asked me to go up and get this out of it. Then she gave it to me."

"Kind old soul," said Sally, remembering all the awful things she had said and thought about Mrs Campbell.

"Yes, she is decent at heart," said Katie. "I'd say the doll is very old. She mumbled something about getting it from some fine lady, a countess or a duchess or something, when she was a child."

"I knew there was something funny about the dress," said Sally. The doll's dress had a very high waist, the kind that is called empire line. Those dresses had been in the fashion about seventy or eighty years ago! "It's a wonder it lasted so long."

"It was all wrapped up in tissue and mothballs, that's why," said Katie. "Even so the dress is very thin and delicate. See?" Katie picked up the hem of the dress. The white cloth had yellowed, and the lace edging looked as if it might crumble into dust at any moment. "I'll make you other dresses for her, Janey. We can make lots of dresses from old bits of cloth and she will have a fine big wardrobe."

Janey hugged the doll close to her.

"It's a lovely thing, Katie," said Mrs Gallagher, giving Katie a hug. There were tears in her eyes. She was glad that Janey had got such a beautiful plaything, and moved to see how happy the little doll made her. "And isn't it great to have the two of you home again! I hope we don't have to be separated now for a good long time."

"I hope so too," said Sally, quietly. "It is wonderful to be home. You all look so well. And the house is just as nice as ever, and everything looks perfect."

But everything was not quite perfect, not yet. It was true that Sally was delighted to be home and seeing Janey and her mother filled her with a warm glow of happiness. But there was somebody else on her mind too, and somebody else she wanted to see very much. It was the thought of that person that cast a slight shadow over the brilliant sunlight of the day and that tinged the joy in her heart with anxiety.

2

Maura

*T*he next day the girls slept late. It was the first morning they had had a chance to do that in months. When Sally came into the kitchen, the fire was leaping on the hearth and her mother was already putting a loaf of bread into the hanging pot to bake over the fire. Janey was at the table, playing with her doll. Rain beat against the window-pane.

Sally made some tea and had it with a slice of bread and butter.

"Like some, mother?" she asked.

"Dead with tea and dead without it!" said her mother. "I might as well. I'm not going to get much done today, that's for sure. No earthly good in putting out the wash. Though God knows I shouldn't be complaining, this is the first drop of rain we've had in weeks. Pray that it lasts a while even if I don't get the washing done at all."

"No," said Sally. "Sure it's Wednesday anyway."

"I didn't get it done on Monday. That's what happens if you don't do things on the right day. There's a time for everything."

"Oh well," said Sally, looking out the window at the

11

greyness and listening to the beating rain. She wondered how she would get through the day, closed up in the house. It seemed very small and confined after the big Stewart farmhouse. And she was wondering when she would meet Manus, the boy she had been seeing on and off over the past couple of years. He was Maura McLoughlin's brother, and she'd sent a letter to Maura telling her when she was coming home. She had half-hoped – no, she had hoped – when she wrote that letter that Maura would tell Manus about it.

Her mother sensed that Sally was worried, although she did not know why. She knew her daughter had gone to a few dances with that McLoughlin boy, as she called him, and she suspected she had some notions about him. But she had no idea of how attached to him Sally had become. In her opinion her daughter, now almost sixteen years of age, was a child, and far too young to have any serious concern with boys. Anyway Sally had always been brainy and a day-dreamer, more interested in reading a book than in hanging about with young lads. In Mrs Gallagher's view, women who read books never had any interest in men. Look at schoolteachers. They seldom married. Happier to live with their books and the schools and their finicky little ways. And as well off too, Mrs Gallagher thought.

Mrs Gallagher assumed that Sally felt out of place at home after such a long time among strangers.

"Have you any plans for today yourself?" she asked kindly. "Maybe you could drop in on Miss Lynch and see if she has any nice books she could lend you?"

That had been Sally's greatest treat when she'd been younger: borrowing books from her old teacher, Miss Lynch. And reading them, of course.

"I might do that," said Sally thoughtfully. The prospect

of visiting Miss Lynch did not seem all that exciting to her now. "I suppose I might call over to see Maura McLoughlin as well. Is she at home now?"

"Och yes, I saw her on Sunday at Mass. She's gone a bit fat, but she was looking lovely, I must say. She's a great girl for the style nowadays, Maura. They're doing well."

"How's that?"

"They've borrowed money from the government and are buying out that big farm of theirs."

"Can you borrow money from the government to do that?"

"You can of course. If you've got the money to pay them back."

"And they have?"

"They have. They're making a great go of old Hughie's shop since they bought that. On borrowed money too. You won't know the place at all now. McLoughlin has built on bits here and bits there and he's got the whole place stocked out with the devil knows what. You'd wonder who buys it all. Sure nobody around here has two pennies to rub together and after last year's desperate harvest they're worse off than ever. But somebody must have money all right. He's a big bucko now, the same McLoughlin."

"Hm," Sally felt worried. She did not want the McLoughlins to get too well off. If that happened they mightn't want to be friends with her. "Well, I'll go over and see what the place looks like, then. Maybe there are all sorts of changes there too?"

"Och, I don't think you'll see many changes in the house. Maybe I'm wrong but I'd say most of the changes are in the shop and on the farm. They've a new thrasher, I've heard, and two horses, if you don't mind. That'll be the changes."

Sally munched her bread morosely.

"I suppose we should think about what I'm to do next?"

Already she suspected that she might find it hard to sit around at home for an indefinite period.

"Och, sure you're hardly inside the door. Have a wee holiday first, then we can start thinking about all that. I've plenty for you to be doing around the place here anyway for the minute, and there'll be more in a month's time."

"I suppose so," said Sally. "I don't like to be idle, that's all. I'm used to being a working girl now."

"You won't be idle around here, my girl," said her mother firmly. "No need to worry about that."

After dinner, the meal of potatoes and milk which they ate at one o'clock, Sally set off to visit Maura. The rain had eased off by then, and the sun shone thinly through the clouds, glancing off the brambles and making the puddles on the dirt road gleam. Sally wore a pair of big old boots as protection against the mud. Her mother had insisted that she put them on. Her blue skirt, which reached to mid-calf, did not cover them up at all. She hoped she wouldn't meet Manus now: she didn't want him to see her in these big ugly boots. Maybe she would take them off as soon as she reached Maura's house, and walk around barefoot inside. Barefoot wasn't ideal either, but anything would look better than the boots. And her feet were nice and clean. She'd given them a rub with a wet cloth before she left the house.

The McLoughlin house was not a one-storey dwelling, like the Gallaghers', but a two-storey house, made of dark grey stones. It had a new slated roof, and, with its three windows upstairs, and big chimney, looked very imposing. It was the sort of house you might expect to have a garden in front. But it didn't. Instead it had the sort of yard that all the houses had, with chickens rooting in it, and old bits of farm machinery here and there.

Sally knocked on the door and then went into the kitchen, which was at the front of the house. It was a much bigger room than the kitchen in her own house. The walls were half timbered in wood, painted green, with the top part of the wall white. There was more furniture in it, too: a big table, half a dozen chairs and stools, a huge brown dresser, and red chests containing grain, meal for the hens. The McLoughlins' dog, Shep, was lying in front of the fire and there was a cat sitting on the window-sill, soaking up the sun. The McLoughlins' house had a funny smell. Sally recalled this as soon as she walked in the door. Also, it always seemed untidy to her after the spick and span conditions of home.

Maura and her mother were there, and one of the men they hired to help on the farm. He was sitting at the back of the room, shovelling potatoes into his mouth. The potatoes were in a pot placed on top of an upturned basket which served him instead of a table. There were potato skins on the floor at his feet. Maura was sitting at the big table under the window, eating bread and jam. Mrs McLoughlin was at the fire, her feet touching Shep's back, crocheting a handkerchief. She was well known for her crochet, which she called "flowering".

"God be with you!" said Sally, when she walked in. "How are you all?"

"Sally!" said Maura. She wiped the red jam off her face with the sleeve of her dress. "You're back. How are you?"

"Hello Sally," said Mrs McLoughlin, turning to face her but not getting up from her chair. "You got back from the Lagan. Come in and sit down, like a good girl."

She resumed her crochet.

Sally sat down at the table with Maura.

"So when did you come home?" asked Maura. "Would you like a bit of bread and jam? This jam is delicious, I can't resist it."

"No thanks," said Sally. "We just had the dinner. We got back last night, late yesterday afternoon, in fact."

"You had a nice journey?"

"Oh yes, very nice."

Sally told her something about the trip, and about life in Tyrone. But she did not feel that Maura was terribly interested.

"That's a nice blouse you have on, Maura," she said, finally, in an effort to make conversation that would interest her friend. "Is it new?"

"It's new. Mother got it for me in town last week, you know, in Boylan's Drapery. They've really nice things there, and I need some stuff. We're going on a holiday."

"A holiday?"

Nobody in Glenbra had ever gone on a holiday. Even in Tyrone, Sally had never heard of anyone having a holiday.

"Yes. We're going to Bundoran for a few days, to visit my aunt. She owns a guest house there, didn't you know? Miss Wilson's 'Railway View'. We'll stay with her and have a holiday. It's a holiday resort, you know, Bundoran, I'm really looking forward to it very much."

"It sounds exciting," said Sally. "When are you going?"

"August," Maura answered. "First week in August. That's the best time for holidays."

"Yes," said Sally. "I'm sure it is. Listen, Maura, would you like to have a little walk? It's cleared up now, we could stroll over to the village."

"Too far," said Maura. "I can't walk that far. My new

16

shoes, they kill me." She stuck her feet out in front of her to show Sally. She had black shoes with a strap across the instep, and buttons at the side. The heels were thick but high.

"What lovely shoes!" said Sally. "But they're not for walking in. Don't you have boots?"

"Wouldn't be seen dead in them!" said Maura. Sally felt uncomfortable, and glanced down at the monstrosities on her own feet. She had felt too shy to remove them after all. Maura was looking at them too.

"So, will you come for a short walk?" Sally wanted to get away from Mrs McLoughlin, who was crocheting away diligently but listening to everything the girls were saying.

"It has to be short," said Maura, sticking her chin in the air. "But I might as well get a bit of fresh air while the rain is holding off. Wait a minute and I'll get my shawl."

"I'll wait in the street," said Sally. "Goodbye, Mrs McLoughlin."

"Goodbye," said Mrs McLoughlin, not looking up. To Maura she said: "Don't be long, dear, I need you in half an hour."

When they were walking along the lane, Maura hobbling a bit in her fine shoes, Sally asked:

"Are you all going to Bundoran so?" It was the only way she could manage to drag Manus into the conversation without directly mentioning him.

"All of us," said Maura. "Oh yes, me and mother and father and Manus and Jimmie and Margaret and wee Mollie. We'll all go, of course."

This did not get her very far.

"Well, what has been going on here? Tell me all the news. Have there been any good dances, or parties, or anything?"

"Oh you know how boring it is around here. Not a thing happens. I can't wait to get way from it. I'll die of boredom if I don't get out soon. But I will."

"You will?"

"Yes, I will, oh yes." Maura pulled her shawl over her forehead, covering most of her thick red hair. "I'll be going away in September, to boarding school. You know, I'll go to the convent in Letterkenny, where Eileen Carr goes now. Daddy wants me to and he can afford it now."

"You are lucky," said Sally, sighing very quietly. She would have loved to go to the convent but that was never going to happen now.

"Oh yes, absolutely wonderful. I have to have a winter dress and a summer dress, six white starched collars, six pairs of drawers, three shifts, three pairs of black stockings, two pairs of white stockings, a red sash for Sundays, and the Lord knows what else. And it is a great school, Eileen says. It's a castle, really, with hundreds of beautiful rooms and huge grounds. I'll play tennis, can you imagine, and learn to play the piano, and speak French and do drawing. And on Saturdays they have dancing lessons. Eileen has been taking them for a year, she is such a terrific dancer, I have never seen anyone who is quite as good a dancer as Eileen. You remember Eileen, don't you?"

"Yes," said Sally. "I've only been gone for a year, of course I remember her."

Eileen Carr was the daughter of the doctor who lived in the next village on from Glenbra. She had not gone to Glenbra school, but to the school in the next parish. For the last two years she had been a boarder at the convent, even though she was about the same age as Maura and Sally. Maura was very old to be starting at the convent,

Sally reflected. Most girls went when they were twelve. She wondered if her friend would find it as nice as she thought, starting so much later than everyone else.

"She is such a lovely girl, you would not believe it. I didn't even like her, or think she was pretty, until this year. But she has improved so much, she is really a friendly person, and looks gorgeous. She wears her hair up, even. She has the loveliest fair hair, and the most perfect silk dress I have ever seen in my whole life."

Sally found all this terribly interesting. She hadn't even known that Maura had ever been inside Eileen Carr's house, a big white house with a long avenue leading up to it from high iron gates, perched down on the edge of the lough, so that it would have a fine view of the sea.

"Do you see much of her, then?" she asked. "Do you visit her or what?"

"Oh yes," said Maura, turning. "We should be getting back now. I'm tired." They had only walked about half a mile and the weather was really fine now. Sally would have loved to continue, and hear more and more on this subject.

"Yes," said Maura, as they walked back towards the house. "I see her all the time, you know. She had a dance at Easter, an Easter party. The whole sitting-room was done up, she had daffodils and a yellow table cloth and everything, and we ate heaps of chocolate eggs. Have you ever had a chocolate egg?"

"No," said Sally. At Easter in Glenbra everyone ate lots of real eggs, saved up from the hens throughout Lent. The children took cans of eggs, bread and butter, and went up to the hills and built a little toy house, called an Easter house. They had a picnic there, and played games, rolling hard-boiled eggs down the hill to see whose egg would win the race. In Tyrone, Easter had been celebrated in a similar fashion. There had been no chocolate eggs, or any other sort of chocolate, there.

"You have never in your life tasted anything so divine. I could eat a dozen chocolate eggs! I did eat two. Eileen gave me most of hers, she didn't want it for some reason. Too busy dancing with Manus, probably."

Maura did not indicate that she thought Sally would have the slightest interest in Manus. Sally looked at her in surprise. Surely she remembered? But surely she would not tell her something like this if she did?

"Manus?" she said. To her surprise, she found that she was shaking. She could hardly pronounce the word.

"Yes, Manus. He and Eileen are the best of friends. He danced with her all evening at the party. He thinks her hair is gorgeous. And her dress. She had the most heavenly silk dress."

"Yes, you said that before," said Sally. She was feeling cross and gloomy.

They had reached the McLoughlins' house. Maura asked Sally if she would like to come in and eat some raisin bread her mother had made that morning, but Sally said no, she had to be getting home.

"Come back tomorrow!" Maura smiled, as she pulled down her shawl and exposed her brilliant red hair to the light of day. "It's really nice that you are back."

"I'll see you soon again," said Sally. She turned and plodded out of the farmyard. Her boots thudded against the ground, splashing in the puddles, repeating "where's Manus where's Manus where's Manus where's Manus."

3

Talking Things Over

*A*fter she left Maura, Sally did not go straight home. Mrs McLoughlin's chilly manners, Maura's chatter about the new school and Eileen Carr, and Manus's absence, had combined to make her feel mixed up and miserable. She decided to walk to the McLoughlins' shop and call on Manus herself.

Full of determination, she strode along the lanes. She paid no attention to the muddy water that splashed her ankles as she plunged into puddle after puddle. She didn't see the valley, spreading in front of her, a plaid of golden, brown and green fields stretching from the hills to the sea; her mind was on other things, concentrating entirely on the meeting ahead.

Occasionally she met people on the road and she had to nod or smile at them. But she avoided stopping to talk, even though everyone was dying to chat to her and find out all about her travels. Once, about half way to the shop, she was forced to stop. She heard a child screaming from the side of the road. When she investigated she found a little boy, whom she recognised as Dónal Greene. He had

21

fallen into a well and was soaked to the skin. Sally pulled him out and brought him back to his mother, Bridgie, a widow who lived in a small cottage with about half a dozen children.

"Is it yourself Sally?" she asked, taking Dónal and shaking him. She did not seem too worried about his escapade; it was the sort of thing he did all the time. "Home from the wars. Won't you come in for a cup of tea?"

But Sally wouldn't.

"I'm in a hurry, I'm afraid," she said as patiently as she could. "I'll call in some other day that I'm passing, thanks all the same."

She was standing in the doorway of the Greene's cottage. It was a grim looking place: one room with no furniture except for an upturned potato creel and a few tiny stools, one bed in the corner. Bridgie Greene was very poor indeed.

"Take care of yourself, Dónal!" she called to him, as she set off again. Quite soon she arrived in the village and she quickly made her way to the McLoughlins' shop.

Her mother was right. It had changed a lot. The house that contained the shop had been whitewashed and painted. Some groceries were displayed in its window and a variety of objects were hanging from hooks on either side of the door: hanks of rope, rubber boots, buckets, fishing nets, reaping hooks. At the side of the house a big red wooden extension had been built. Someone was unloading sacks of guano from a cart onto the ground outside and another man was carrying them into the store.

Sally gazed at the shop. Now that she was here she did not feel so brave all of a sudden. She wished very much that she had a few pence in her pocket. Then at least she would have had a good excuse for going into the shop.

But she hadn't a farthing.

She walked up and peeped in through the window.

She couldn't see much. The shop was even more cluttered up with things inside than outside. Every available bit of space seemed to have something hanging out of it. But she could catch a glimpse of the counter. Behind it was Mr McLoughlin, wearing a brown coat. There was no sign of Manus.

"Well, you've come here now," Sally said to herself. "You have to go in." She took a deep breath and counted to five. Then she pushed in the door of the shop. A bell rang as soon as she did this.

"Good day," Mr McLoughlin was pouring sugar into brown bags. He did not look up when Sally entered.

Sally breathed deeply again. Her knees were shaking.

"Hello," she said. The simple word came out as a tinny frightened croak.

"Can I help you?" he looked up now but he did not seem to recognise her.

"Em," said Sally. "Em . . . "

He waited. His face was floury grey.

"I wondered . . . would Manus be here?"

Mr McLoughlin glanced at her and his eyes narrowed.

"No," he said. His voice was flat. He's not here today."

Sally's stomach felt punctured. She waited for Mr McLoughlin to say something else. But he didn't. He yawned and went back to scooping bags of sugar.

"Goodbye then," she left the shop. Ting a ling!

"You shouldn't have done it!" Sally berated herself. She was swamped by a sour mixture of disappointment and shame. "Why did you do it? Stupid, stupid." Then she started to feel annoyed at Mr McLoughlin. Couldn't he have been a bit nicer? Couldn't he have at least told her where Manus had gone?

She was walking slowly along the village street, lost in these unpleasant thoughts, when someone tapped her on the shoulder. She jumped in shock.

It was Miss Lynch.

"Ah! Miss Lynch! How are you?"

"Hello Sally. It's wonderful to see you! So you've come home?"

"Yes," said Sally, trying to collect herself. "Yes I've come home. Yesterday, I think. Yesterday, we came home."

She smiled and began to feel a bit more normal. Miss Lynch was one of those people who can put everyone at their ease. She reminded Sally of warm delicious things. Fresh loaves of bread. Soup on a cool day. Even though she dressed in cool colours – white lace blouse, pale blue skirt – she looked like a warm person.

"Why don't you come in and have a chat? I'm just out of school. Won't you have something to eat with me?"

Sally hesitated for a second. In a way she would have liked to be alone, to be miserable in peace and quiet. But she did not want to be impolite. And she knew she would feel much better after a chat with Miss Lynch if she could just let herself enjoy it.

"All right," she said. "Thanks very much."

Miss Lynch's house was at the edge of the village. It was a cottage set in a small garden, full, at the moment, of blue delphiniums and yellow wallflowers. Sally followed her into the tiny hall, where Miss Lynch took off her shawl. Then she ushered Sally into a sitting-room. She had never been before. It was almost as she had imagined it must be. A simple whitewashed room, but with a hundred little prettifying touches that gave it character and made it special: there were blue and white check curtains on the windows, and a little sofa and easy chair covered in plain white cloth. There was a wooden bookcase, painted white, and filled with brownbacked volumes. A small oak table with a vase of roses on it, some bright watercolours on the walls – watercolours painted by Miss Lynch herself. In the corner was a small upright piano, with a little label saying "Pohlman and Company Dublin" stuck on it.

"Sit down, dear," said Miss Lynch. "I won't be a minute with the lunch."

Sally was just going to say that she'd already had dinner, but bit the words back.

She sat down on the sofa while Miss Lynch moved around fetching things from the kitchen.

"How well you are looking, Sally!" she said putting a plate of cake on the table. "And are you home for good now, or will you go back to Tyrone again?"

"No," said Sally. "The answer is no to both questions, really. I don't want to go back to Tyrone, if I can help it, and I don't want to stay here either."

"No?" Miss Lynch sounded surprised.

"No. I want to get another job somewhere else. I think I'd like to work in a town for a while, just to see what that was like."

"It could be very different from what you are used to. How is your mother?"

"Oh, she seems to be doing well now. You know she has managed to keep the rent paid, and until this winter she seemed to be doing very well. She was thinking of starting to buy the place out. But now there is no chance of that, with the bad harvest last year."

"It has been hard on everyone. It seems that half the

parish has gone to America."

"Yes. So I've heard. Mother was saying that Elizabeth Greene and Mary Martin both left last week."

"That's right. They've gone to Canada, not to America. I was at the party for them in Martin's house a week last Thursday. They were taking the boat at Derry, the *White Star* line."

"Anyone who can afford to goes, don't they? Mother was telling me that they're giving away farms in Canada to anyone who will take them. Maybe that's what I should do."

"Och, Sally, they won't give you a farm! Anyway you don't want to live in the North West Territory, you'd freeze."

"You can get land in British Columbia too. That'd be a warm place, wouldn't it?"

"Warm and far away. Those farms are for families anyway. You'd have to get married first."

"Not much chance of that around here."

Miss Lynch ignored this.

"It's such a pity you can't continue school. You'd be a great teacher."

"Well, there's no chance of that either. Mother needs all the help she can get," said Sally. "I'm too old anyway. I'll be sixteen in no time at all. Nobody starts back to school at my age. Except Maura. Maura is going to the convent in September."

"Yes. Maura is lucky. Not that she is very interested in studying, but she will enjoy other things the convent has to offer."

"She'll enjoy all the clothes."

"Yes. And she won't enjoy all the watery cabbage and porridge, which is mainly what you get to eat at that convent. Don't envy her too much!"

"Oh dear, no. I do envy her a bit, though."

"That's to be expected, I suppose. Come over to the table now and have something to eat."

Sally joined Miss Lynch at the little table.

"Would you have some seed cake? Some shortbread?"

"I'll have a piece of shortbread, thanks very much. Yes, and some tea, that would be lovely."

Miss Lynch was eating oaten bread and rhubarb jam.

"I can understand that you would have liked to have her opportunities, but that's not how life is. You will always do well with your own, whatever happens."

"Maura seems to – I don't know – not be interested in knowing me any more, I suppose." Sally did not know why she blurted this out. She had had some conversations with Miss Lynch before, but she had never confided anything really important or personal to her. However, she felt she had to talk to somebody.

"How is that?" asked Miss Lynch.

"I've just been over at her house. Her mother didn't say a word to me, acted as if I wasn't worth talking to. And Maura wasn't very friendly either, I thought. She seemed to be showing off all the time, trying to say things that would impress and annoy me at the same time."

"Hm," said Miss Lynch. "And that surprises you?"

"Yes, of course it surprises me. She was my best friend once, you know."

"Time has passed. People change, especially at the age you and Maura are at. Some mature faster than others. It is normal to grow away from someone you used to be fond of when you were younger."

"Well, Maura and I haven't much in common any more, that's certainly true. I'm a hired girl and she is a rich shopkeeper's daughter now. She's going to school. She's even going on a holiday to Bundoran, to a house called 'Railway View'. Imagine that!"

"It's not just things like that. Anyway, you shouldn't expect everybody to like you. I expect most people with any sense would. But some people don't have any sense. Maura might be envious of you too, you know."

"I can't imagine why."

"No, but I can see it easily. Money and new clothes are not everything. You shouldn't start imagining that they are. What are your own immediate plans? Are you staying here for a while?"

"Probably. Mother wants me to stay for the rest of the summer. She needs help with this and that, we're having a visitor coming next month to stay with us. You know, a paying visitor. She's coming here to learn Irish."

"Ah yes, I've heard about that. Glenbra is starting to be on the tourist map all of a sudden. You should stay here, Sally, because other interesting things will happen here soon, just wait and see."

"Oh, such as?"

"Well, in September, for instance, classes will start in the old schoolhouse, to teach girls and women here, girls really, how to crochet."

"You mean, like Mrs McLoughlin?"

"Yes. Only you would learn all kinds of complicated stitches, and how to make lots of things, not just the little handkerchiefs. Then this person will arrange for you to sell them to shops in Scotland and Dublin. You would learn a skill and then you could earn some money with it. Do you think that would interest you?"

"Oh dear," said Sally. "I don't know. I mean it sounds like a fine idea and everything. But I hate knitting and sewing and all that stuff, you know. Katie, now, is good at that sort of thing. She has patience. But I haven't. I'd much rather read a book, or write a letter, or even pull a field of spuds, you know. I like to do things quickly."

"Well, you might be right about yourself. But it is something to think about. You can tell me if you feel like going to the classes, and tell Katie about them too, and anyone else you know. We want a good number. It's part of a new scheme to help people in this part of the country, organised by something called the 'Congested Districts Board'."

"What a funny name. What is a congested district?"

"Glenbra is. It means there are a lot of people and not enough work or money to go around. Congested in that way."

"I'm feeling congested myself, after that shortbread," said Sally. "It was so good. But I had a big feed of potatoes only a while ago, so I'm stuffed."

"Goodness, Sally. I've never heard you make a joke before."

"Was that a joke?"

"Yes. Now, do you want to wash your hands before you go?"

"Excuse me?"

Miss Lynch laughed.

"My turn to joke. I just want to show off my new bathroom. Have you ever seen one before?"

"No," said Sally. "I never have."

"Come this way and I'll show you."

Miss Lynch went across the room and through the door. Sally followed her. There was a tiny passageway there with two doors opening off. Miss Lynch opened one of them.

"That's it!" she said.

It was a very small bathroom, containing a big white bath with claw feet, a washhand basin and a large toilet with a huge iron chain dangling from a cistern above it.

"This is how you use the wash basin," Miss Lynch demonstrated, turning on and off a tap. "And this is how you flush the lavatory." She pulled the chain. Sally started in fright at the sound of water crashing down from the cistern.

"It's very nice," she said, politely, privately thinking that it was very alarming indeed. "When did you get it?"

"In April. A man from Enniskillen came and put it in. Isn't it just wonderful? I'll leave you here for a minute and you can try it out."

"Oh, really, it is not . . . "

Sally did not want to be left alone in this room. But already Miss Lynch had vanished, shutting the door behind her.

She did not dare try out the toilet. She guessed what it was for but she couldn't imagine actually sitting on such a contraption. She examined the contents of a small shelf above the hand-basin: it was filled with little bottles and jars. "Crabapple Perfume. Coyles of Covent Garden" was one bottle. "Eppel's Pills. Best for all Female Complaints" was another. There was a jar labelled "Cold Cream" and several tin boxes of ointments and lotions which were familiar to Sally. She opened the bottle of perfume and smelled it, but did not dab a bit on her wrists. Then she decided to try to turn on a tap. There were two taps on the wash-basin, so she selected one of them. Nothing came out. Then she tried the other. A thick stream of water rushed into the basin. Sally took the bar of soap and rubbed some on her hands. Then she tried to turn off the tap. But she couldn't turn it at all. The water rushed and rushed, and she twisted and twisted but she could not get it to stop.

She rushed out of the bathroom.

"Miss Lynch, Miss Lynch!" she shouted. "I can't turn it off. It won't turn off for me!"

Miss Lynch scurried along and with one deft twist of her fingers stemmed the flow. She smiled sympathetically at Sally. "It takes time to get used to all these modern technical inventions," she said. "But once you do you can't imagine being without them."

Sally thought she could get along without them very well.

4

Mother in Love

*S*ally had been at home for more than a week. The days were full of work and activity and she was kept fully occupied. Her mother wanted to have turf cut, she wanted to dye wool, she wanted to wash the outside of the house with lime in preparation for the arrival of her summer visitor. Sally helped, eagerly enough, with all of this. She went for walks with Katie, and occasionally with Maura. She played with Janey and told her stories. She read a book she had borrowed from Miss Lynch. But all the time she wondered where he was. Not where he was. She knew that. He was in the shop, working with his father. Not behind the counter out in the front where she could have met him, as if by accident, when she went to buy a quarter pound of tea, but behind the scenes in the big warehouse or store they had at the back of the shop. That's where Manus was, according to Maura, from early in the morning until eight or nine o'clock at night. She did not give Sally any hint as to how she might meet him. Sally would have to knock on the door of the store, wait until someone answered it, and ask for Manus by name.

She would never have the courage to do that. Not after her encounter with his father.

She would have to wait for Manus to call on her. He knew where she was. He would have to take the first step.

Sally had never confided much about her feelings for Manus to Katie, mainly because she knew Katie would deride them and tease her about them. But her sister had some inkling of what was going on in Sally's mind. She did think it was all silly and beneath contempt. Really such stupid carry on! But she was not cruel and she had some sympathy with Sally.

"Sure he probably doesn't even know you're here!" she said. "Did you write to him? Did you tell him?"

"No," Sally tossed her head scornfully. The idea!

"So what makes you so sure he knows you're home. Do you think he's divinely inspired or what?"

"Maura would have mentioned it, of course, or even his mother. Sure I've been up at the house two or three times."

"That one! I wouldn't bet tuppence on it. Those McLoughlins are all as sneaky as cats anyway. And they're so full of themselves. I don't know what you see in them at all."

Katie was in a brisk and practical mood. She was busy and she had plans. After two days at home she informed her mother and Sally that she was going to hire herself out again for the summer. It came as a shock to both of them.

"Sure you're hardly in the door," said her mother. "You don't have to go off again, you know. We'll manage well enough the year with what you've earned already, and I'll have money from the visitor now coming and God knows what."

"You're going off on your own?" It was nothing new for Katie to be away from home, working, but hitherto she had always had Sally close by. Sally couldn't believe that she'd voluntarily set off alone. "Are you sure you don't want me to come with you?"

"No," Katie said. "Mother needs one of us here this summer, on account of the summer visitor coming, and I really would rather go away. I'd like to try it, alone, for once."

"Well, I'll go if you want me to," said Sally.

"It's good of you, but I'd prefer it this way."

"You used to be so homesick at the Campbells. Remember you ran away?"

"That was more than a year ago. It's different now. I've decided to go to the hiring fair at Rathmullan next Thursday. I've missed the Milford one and the one in Letterkenny."

"I heard from someone that the wages were low, at Letterkenny. Hardly anyone got hired, they couldn't get enough money. Girls were only getting £5, and men £10."

"I'll do better than that. Anyway, £5 is £5. We need it, especially if the potatoes don't do well this year."

"They'll do well. Everything is doing better than ever, it's not like last summer at all."

"It's too dry, they are saying. But even if everything is fine, and even though we'll have money from the visitor, I want some extra for myself. I want to save a bit of money from now on. I want to have a dowry." She winked at her mother.

"Mm."

"Yes. I have to think about that. What am I going to get married with?"

"Well . . . do you have to start worrying about that now? You are only fourteen."

"I know none of the ones around here get married until

34

they have one foot in the grave, but I want to be ready to do it when I am twenty. Not one day older. That's what I have in mind."

"Sure who'd have you, even with money in the bank?" Sally could not resist teasing Katie, she looked so serious when she said all this.

"Plenty will have her," said Mrs Gallagher. "Don't you worry, they'll have her all right. And it always helps to have something put by. She is right. I don't know what you're hoping for, Miss."

"I've more to worry me than dowries," said Sally, tossing her head.

The talk of dowries made her feel worried. It was not that she had any serious thoughts of marriage. But any mention of it made her think of Manus and Eileen Carr. Eileen Carr! She would have a dowry, if that was something that Manus was worried about. If he cared about dowries, Sally would have to put all thoughts of him right out of her head. No matter what she did she was not going to be able to beat the like of Eileen Carr on the dowry stakes.

"Stop!" Sally said to herself. "Stop thinking about these things. You haven't even seen him in months and months. He has probably forgotten that you even exist. What a waste of time to spend two minutes worrying about him and his dowries. It's all Katie's fault for bringing it up anyway."

The question of marriage was in the air, however, in the household, and it was not easy to avoid it.

This was not owing to Katie at all, but to Mrs Gallagher herself.

She was being courted.

Every evening, almost every evening, Packy Doherty

came calling. So did some other people: Madge Doherty from over the road, Mrs Gallagher's best friend. A few boys from the village who were cousins of Sally and Katie and who spent the summer nights roaming from house to house, céilí-ing. And one or two others. But Packy was the most regular visitor, and he was not a relation at all.

He came at about nine o clock, when the day's work was done. Sally had already learned to recognise his heavy, slow footstep outside the door. Everything about Packy was like that footstep, she thought. Heavy and slow. He raised the latch himself and then entered the kitchen, stooping deeply because he was bigger than the door, and lifting his cap for half a second. He mumbled – slowly – "God bless all here," put his cap back on, and, still bending slightly, went over to the hard chair beside the dresser and sat down.

"Pull up your chair to the fire, man dear," Mrs Gallagher would say. And he would. It annoyed Sally that he never did this without being asked.

He was the tallest man she had ever seen, the brownest, the slowest and the most silent. All night he would sit, from nine until about midnight, without saying a thing. If other people were in, he would nod and laugh at their jokes and stories, and once Sally had heard him saying "Aye, I mind that, I mind that." At midnight, having had tea and bread, he would get up, stretch, and make his exit, mumbling inaudibly "Goodnight to yes now." That was it.

"He's planning to marry Mother," Katie said.

"Packy? Don't be cracked."

"Why would he be coming here every night if he wasn't?"

"Well . . . for the tea?"

"Don't be cracked yourself. He's got his eye on her, it's obvious."

"He's so old."

"Fifty, so they say."

"She wouldn't have him anyway. What would she want with an old fellow like that, who hasn't a tongue in his head? He's not a bit like Daddy."

"No. Still, she might be lonely."

"I suppose she might. But wouldn't she be lonely with him anyway?"

"He's got a good farm. Money too, probably."

"That's all anyone cares about around here."

"They have to care about it."

Sally sighed and said nothing.

"Don't be so high and mighty. It might be a very good thing for Mother, and for all of us, if she married him."

"Och, I don't think it'll ever happen. He'll never manage to get the words out anyway. Sure how would he propose?"

"Oh my dear Mrs Gallagher! I have admired you for so long . . . "

"In silence."

"Would you please consent . . . " Katie got down on her knees. "To be my lawful wedded wife?"

Sally punched her in the tummy, and both girls collapsed giggling on the floor.

Katie and Sally were very busy for the next few days: their mother decided that she would dye several bags of wool that she had been spinning throughout the winter. Now she had hundreds of hanks of white yarn which could be knit into jumpers and socks, or sent to the weaver to be made into cloth. But first Mrs Gallagher wanted to dye it different colours. You could buy aniline dyes in the shop for this purpose, and these gave very brilliant colours, just like the colours of clothes bought in shops in town. But most people in Glenbra still made their own colours at home using flowers, roots, lichens, and other things which they could gather for free in the countryside. Mrs Gallagher always liked to get things for free if at all possible. So for several days, Sally and Katie, and even Janey, were out gathering the materials that would form the basis of the dyestuffs she would use to colour her wool.

First they went up the side of the hill to where there was a large outcrop of rock. On the rock grew a grey lichen, with yellow mixed through it, called "crottle". They scraped it off with kitchen knives and filled a bucket with it. This was very slow work. It was not so hard to scrape the lichens off the rock, but it takes a lot of lichen to fill a bucket, and Mrs Gallagher wanted two bucketfuls, since crottle gave one of the best colours: a dark, rich rust colour. It also happened to be her favourite colour. The girls spent almost two days getting the required amount. They did not mind: the sun shone brilliantly, and it was fun to be out on the hillside, singing, talking, and chipping away at the rocks.

That was the hardest part of the work of gathering. As well as crottle, they gathered meadowsweet from the ditches, but it was easy to pick huge bunches of that, since the ditches were overflowing with it. The meadowsweet, mixed with bog ink, would give a good deep black, from which Mrs Gallagher would get a length of cloth for a skirt for herself. They also gathered ragweed, which would give a yellow dye, and dock leaves, which would give green. They did not get too much of those, because they did not like yellow and green cloth much: people thought it was unlucky, because the fairies wear yellow and green.

What Sally and Katie wanted was red dye.

"You can't have that," said Mrs Gallagher. "The crottle will have to do instead. It is a kind of red anyway."

But there was one thing that would give a better, redder colour than crottle, and that was madder root. So Katie and Sally spent an extra day digging up these roots with a sharp spade.

When the plants and roots and lichens were gathered, another day was spent preparing them. The lichen had to be spread out in the sun to dry, and then crumbled into a powder. After that it had to be left to steep for weeks. The madder root had to be pounded, and the meadowsweet boiled. Mrs Gallagher worked with those straightaway, and soon had some yellow and red wool drying out on the bushes in the yard. The crottle would have to wait for another month.

"Can I get my red cloth made now?" Katie asked.

"I'd rather send it all off together," her mother said. "You know we don't send it to Barney any more. We give it to McLoughlin. He's the agent for the Downings Woollen Company. He'll send it to them and they'll do the weaving for us."

"Why?" asked Sally. "It seems silly to send wool to Downings, when it can be woven here by Barney."

"That's the way it's done now," said Mrs Gallagher. "It's cheaper, and the cloth is made on big mechanical looms in a factory. It wears better."

"What about Barney?"

"Och well, what about him?"

She had to be pleased with that.

5

A Stroke of Fortune

*K*atie, true to her word, went off to the hiring fair at Rathmullan and found a job on a farm in County Derry, near Limavaddy. She set off, herself and another girl and boy, with the farmer who had hired them, and did not shed a tear saying goodbye to Sally, who had come with her to the fair. It was all very different from the scene two years ago when the two girls had waved goodbye to their mother in the diamond at Milford, and all three of them had cried their eyes out.

Sally did not cry this time either. Six months would pass soon enough, she thought: her idea about time had changed over the past couple of years. She did not know where she would be in six months, of course. She had a vague idea that she would not be in Glenbra, but she hadn't a clue as to what she might be doing or where she might be going at any stage in the future. Her mind was full of vague hopefulness. She saw her own future as a broad, straight, sunny road leading to a brilliant horizon. But she had no concrete plans and no idea of where that road was leading.

Sally and Katie had walked to Rathmullan, which was only about five miles from Glenbra, and, when she had left Katie, Sally spent a some time strolling around the streets.

The little seaside town was buzzing with activity today, as hundreds of people thronged it. There were not only those going to the fair to be hired or to hire, but all those who came along with them, and others who came just to see what was going on and to soak up the atmosphere.

There were stalls selling gimcracks and sweets, women with baskets of shellfish and herring, a man selling brogues from a huge basket, a woman with a stall heaped with old clothes. On a patch of green in front of Strand Street a tent was set up. Pies and roast meat, cooked on a fire outside the tent, were available there, 2d for the pies and 4d for a plate of roast beef. It smelled delicious. Sally had a shilling in her pocket and she treated herself to a pie. Biting hungrily into the crispy pastry, filled with minced meat and onions, she continued to stroll around the fair.

On the green beside the food tent some entertainers had assembled. A man wearing a high black hat was doing the three-card trick. The crowd around him eyed him warily and some of the men shouted in angry voices from time to time, when they lost money. Sally stood at the back of the throng. The atmosphere was tense; it felt as if a fight might erupt at any moment. She moved away.

At the other side of the green were two boys doing acrobatics. They were welding themselves into all kinds of shapes, so that they often looked as if they were one person with a lot of arms and legs protruding in this direction and that. You could not really see their two individual faces, but she could make out that one had black hair and the other fair. This was particularly apparent when one of them – the black-haired one – stood on his head, on top of the fair-haired boy's head. Sally had not thought that such a thing was possible. It was such a wonderful feat of balance and strength, even though they held the pose for less than twenty seconds, that the whole crowd burst into tumultuous applause when it was over. The boys bowed and within seconds were tumbling and twisting again.

The sun was beginning to sink a bit in the sky, and Sally decided reluctantly that she should be heading homeward. It would take her almost two hours to complete the long walk. The fair was still in full swing all along the main street of the town, which ran along by the sea. There were even people on the beach, dressed in striped linen dresses and sitting under huge umbrellas. A donkey trotted up and down the sand, giving rides to children, a penny a time. Sally sighed, and wished she could spend more time here, and regretted not having brought Janey along. She decided that the next time there was a fair here, and there would be in less than a month, she would bring her little sister along. Janey was strong enough to walk the five miles now, although she would find it a bit far. Maybe they could arrange some sort of lift? Didn't Packy Doherty own a horse?

Sally was considering these aspects of her next visit to the town when another tent caught her eye: a bright yellow tent. She could hardly have avoided seeing it. It was a tall, conical tent, of a shape she had never seen before, and of the brightest colour imaginable, so brilliant that it seemed to cast its own light on the grass surrounding it. A large paper sign fluttered on a tree just at the side of the tent: "Fortune Teller" it said, in red letters. "Madame Rosa Lee. Palms Read for 3 pence. Crystal Ball 6 pence. 100 per cent correct. Scientifically proven."

The flap of the tent was closed so you could not see inside. Sally stood for a long time looking at it, wondering if Madame Rosa Lee would come out. She read the sign three times, and fingered the coins in her pocket. She had a threepenny bit and one sixpence, even though she had bought some sugar o' candy for Janey, who had managed to devour all the sweets she had from Tyrone long ago. Would it be a sinful waste to have her fortune told? She could imagine what her mother would say.

She was just about to walk away when the flap of the tent moved and a woman emerged.

She was tall and dark, almost black. Her hair was a black ball of wool, and was decorated with golden ornaments in the shape of snakes. She was dressed in flame coloured silk, or satin, some very shiny material: a long draped robe, with golden braid on the edges. On the silk was embroidered one big golden dragon.

"You want your fortune told?" the woman – it was Madame Rosa – asked.

"Yes," said Sally, although five seconds before she had decided she did not.

"Good, follow me please."

Madame Rosa spoke in a very low but penetrating voice. She did not speak like anyone Sally had ever heard before, not like people in Donegal or Tyrone or Derry. Obviously she was foreign. Maybe she was African? Maybe she was one of the heathens Sally had heard so much about? She began to feel a bit frightened. But she followed the woman into the tent.

Inside, the tent was hung with paper decorations of the kind people used at Christmas: chains of blue and red tissue paper. There were also a number of coloured pictures of the Sacred Heart and the Child of Prague stacked up on the floor, and a basket full of clothes pegs. Sally understood from this that when she was not telling fortunes Madame Rosa worked as a pedlar of holy pictures and clothes pegs. This did not worry her too much.

Madame Rosa sat on a hard chair at one side of a small table, which was draped with a crimson cloth, and indicated to Sally that she should sit opposite, on a wooden stool. Sally sat down.

"Palm or Ball?" asked Madame Rosa.

"Palm."

"Or Cards," added Madame Rosa. "Cards 2 pence only."

"Palm," said Sally, who did not like to change her mind once she had decided on something.

"Hold out palm," said Madame Rosa.

Sally held out her palm, and Madame Rosa took it in her large brown hand. She stared at it for a long time, with an anxious look on her face.

"Ah yes," she said, after about five minutes, looking Sally in the eye. Then she stooped to examine the palm again.

"Ah yes," she said. "You have suffered much, and you will suffer much more. You have a great ability to suffer."

Sally felt terrible, but she did not say anything.

"It is a gift, a great gift. You have a great ability to be happy too. You will feel in your life great joy and great sorrow. That is what is in store for you. I see a long life. See," she pulled Sally's hand and showed it to her. "This is the life line. That is very long. You will live to be very very old, I do not know how long exactly, maybe ninety years of age, maybe a hundred and five, it is not clear. Ninety five, I think, most likely. Yes.

"And this," she yanked up Sally's hand again, and showed her another line, "is the travel line. You have travelled a lot already, I read here. Is it true?"

"Yes" said Sally. "I've been to Tyrone. Twice."

"You will travel much more. You will . . . cross water. Yes, that is not so clear. It is not clear if you will cross water or not. You may travel a lot and not cross water."

"How could I do that?"

Madame Rosa looked annoyed. "Do not ask me. It is what the palm says, not me. You could travel to Cork, I think, or Dublin, maybe. Have you been to Derry?"

"No."

"Derry. Maybe that is what it is saying. Maybe it is saying that you will go to Canada or Americay or Scotland too. It is blurred. The line is blurred. But you are going to travel somewhere, and that is going to change your life. You are going to be a rich woman before you die. Very wealthy. I see that. You will be richer than a queen."

"Hm," said Sally.

"Richer than the Queen of England," said Madame Rosa, warming to this theme. "Richer than the King of England too. Richer than the King of Portugal, where I come from, I, Madame Rosa Lee De Largo. Yes. And finally," said Madame Rosa, "what you are waiting for. The heart line. Am I not right?"

Sally nodded.

"Ah, yes," said Madame Rosa. She sighed and bowed her head. "Ah yes. You will love more than one man. More than one man will love you. I see great sorrow and great joy. I see a dark man and a fair man. You will love both of them but they will not both love you."

"Which one will love me?" asked Sally, tentatively.

"It is not clear. The line is blurred. You will marry twice. That is clear. Maybe not to these men. You will have six children, three when you are young and three when you are older. One of them will cause you great sorrow. One of them will break your heart. But you will be rich. You will live in a big house and have your own maids. That's it. That will be threepence please."

Sally gave her the threepence and left the tent.

6

Acrobat

Sally came out of the tent, blinking in the sunshine. She had been inside the little yellow enclosure for about fifteen minutes, but it had seemed like much more. She could hardly believe that it was still light outside, that the grass was green, that the town was on her left hand side, still buzzing with the bustle of the fair, and that to the north was the road that wound along the shore until it came to Glenbra. Madame Rosa's tent had been like another planet, a magical mysterious place. The crimson cloth, the crystal ball, the lamp flickering against the yellow walls of the tent, had made a strong impression on Sally, as strong as the strange and terrifying things that Madame Rosa had told her.

Nonsense. All ould nonsense. That's what Mrs Gallagher would say. Sally had no intention of telling her what she had been doing.

She rubbed her eyes and began to walk homeward.

But she had hardly gone more than a few yards when she heard someone coming along behind her.

She turned. It was the boy from the fair, the acrobat

47

with the yellow hair. He was still dressed as he had been for his act, in white trousers and a white shirt: Sally had seen that much of him. He was running and bounding along the road, taking a hop and a skip, occasionally turning a cartwheel as he came.

She stood and watched for a moment: he was a remarkable sight, in his white clothes, spinning along the road against the backdrop of the clear blue sky and blue sea. She would have liked to gaze at him for longer, but was embarrassed to do so. She turned her face homeward once again, and set off at a brisk pace.

But he was catching up on her. Even though she did not look back, she could hear him drawing closer. She could hear his feet occasionally striking the dry clay road, she could hear stones that he flicked out of his way, then she felt a little breeze and the next minute he went cartwheeling past her, his white clothes flapping in the air.

He landed on his feet just a couple of yards in front of Sally and waited for her.

"Hello," he said, as she walked towards him. "I am Olafur the Human Cartwheel. You can call me Olaf. Who are you?"

"Sally Gallagher," said Sally.

"Where are you going?"

"I am going home," she said, not sure if she should say it or not.

"I'll walk along the way with you if I may. I'm going that way too."

"Well . . ."

"I live out here. For the moment, I live out here, along this road, a bit along the way. I'll just wheel myself along with you, if you don't mind. I get bored, spinning along on my own."

"Where's your friend?"

"He's got business at the fair. Michael O'Sullivan. That's my friend, Michael O'Sullivan. He's seeing a man about a torch. He wants to eat fire as soon as possible."

"Is that what you do all the time, go around to fairs and do tricks and so on?"

"And so on and so forth. That is our profession, that is our game. At the moment. I have other ambitions, much grander, much much grander, than that."

"What are they?"

"I do not think I know you well enough to tell you. Do you think I know you well enough?"

"It's up to you, I suppose. Where are you from anyway? You are not from around here. You sound different."

"Ah, you notice. Can you guess where I'm from?"

"No. I've never heard anyone who sounded like you before. You're not from the north at all, are you? You must be from the south of Ireland somewhere. Are you from Cork?"

"I am not."

"Kerry, then, maybe?"

"I am from the north. I am an Icelander."

"A what?"

"I come from Iceland. Have you not heard of Iceland?"

"I have heard of it. But I've never met someone from there before. I thought Eskimos lived in Iceland."

Olaf laughed. "There are no Eskimos in Iceland. Only Icelanders. People like me."

"You look just . . . "

"Like anyone else. Yes. We look like anyone from Ireland or England or Scotland or Norway, and we are like them too."

"How did you get here anyway?"

"On a fishing boat. Icelandic boats come here quite frequently. Mine has been docked in Killybegs all summer. I left it a few weeks ago."

"I see. You wanted to try something new."

"Yes. I wanted to try something new. Only it is not new. In Iceland I have also done this thing, with my friend, Bjarni. Then I found a boy in Killybegs, Michael, and he is also good at acrobatic things. So we have moved around together. We go to the hiring fairs, and the horse fairs, and the cattle fairs, the butter fairs, and the saint's day fairs, and all the other fairs."

"Do you earn a lot of money?"

"Enough."

"And where do you stay? Do you have a tent, like Madame Rosa Lee?"

"Ah, not like Madame Rosa. No, we have not got a tent. Sometimes we sleep out under the stars. It has been a fine summer. Most of the time I do that. Sometimes I go to a house, I ask for a night's lodging. They always say yes. They are not unkind, people in this district, I have found. They are rather like Icelandic people in that way too."

"You have good English."

"You too have good English. You are an English speaker?"

"Not really. I am an Irish speaker. But I have learned English at school, and I have worked away from home where they spoke English. It is not so hard, I find. But in Iceland do you speak English?"

"No. In Iceland we speak Icelandic. But I have learned English in Killybegs and in other places I have been. And now I will learn Irish too, I think. Sally. So, Sally, where is home? Are we there soon?"

They had not covered much ground.

"No. It's about another four miles. Three or four miles. I will go along this road for four miles and then I will be home. It is simple enough."

"I will go with you for one more mile, and then I will go back to this town. I must meet Michael and see if he has got the torches. I too will eat fire."

"Tomorrow there is no fair . . . where will you go then?"

"Oh, I do not know. We will stay there for a while, maybe. There are people in Rathmullan, you know, all the time. They are going to bathe in the sea, and go for walks, and have holidays. We stay a little while. Then we find another hiring fair, maybe, or some other fair. We can go back to Killybegs, and to Bundoran. Good places for us."

"Yes. They would be. Buncrana too. You could go across the lough to Buncrana, and do your tricks there."

"Where is that?"

"Just across there. See."

Sally pointed across the inlet of water to a cluster of grey houses on the edge of the shore.

"Ah yes. That is a resort, too?"

"Yes, it is. And it is easy to get across. You get a boat at the pier in Rathmullan. My sister went across today."

"You have a sister. Brothers and sisters? A big family?"

Sally told him about Janey, and her father's death.

"That is sad. Your mother should marry somebody else. That happened to my father too. He died. He was out looking for sheep in the winter and he got lost. Died. Cold, you know. It is cold in Iceland in the winter, we have lots of snow. We found him in the spring buried in a snowdrift. My mother married again, another sheep farmer. It is too hard for a woman to be alone on a farm. Your mother is on a farm?"

"Yes."

"It is hard work. You help?"

"I help, when I am there."

"I can help too, maybe, if I am there. I will come when you are harvesting the potatoes. I will come in August. There will be a feast day then I think? Blaeberry Sunday, is that not what they call it? And in Rathmullan, a big fair, a regatta. I and Michael will be here for that, eating fire and spinning wheels. Then I will help your mother pick the spuds."

"You are welcome," said Sally, laughing uneasily.

"So, where do you live? How will I find the place?"

She gave him directions.

"Now I will go back. Goodbye, Sally. It was nice to meet you."

"Goodbye," said Sally.

He did one cartwheel, and then he ran off at top speed away from her down the road.

7

Manus

*I*t is strange, Sally thought, that it was just after her meeting with the Icelander on the road from Rathmullan that Manus turned up on her doorstep again. It was not that she had taken any particular fancy to Olaf. He was such a strange fellow that that was very unlikely to happen. But his very strangeness had affected her and cast her into a new way of thinking. The image of him tumbling along the road like some great wild swan, and the image of dusky Madame Rosa, were together in her mind, two sides of a coin. It seemed to her that Madame Rosa, for all her silk wraps and golden jewellery, her exotic black skin, was in some ways just like Mrs Gallagher. She was kind and she meant well. But she was intent on handing Sally a life of responsibilities; she was impressing on her how difficult everything had to be. It was as if they both felt it was their duty to pass on this sad burden of knowledge to Sally, to warn her that life was a minefield to be crossed with caution.

Olaf hadn't told her anything about life. But just being with him lightened her attitude to it. There he was, a fisherman from Iceland, travelling from fair to fair in Donegal as if it were the easiest most natural thing in the world. Sleeping under the stars, because the weather was fine. Sleeping in some stranger's house if it were not. Sally knew she could never be like Olaf. She would always sleep in a house, and worry about the future, and think about having enough food and enough money for the rent. About having a dowry! Imagine Katie, on her way to Limavaddy, working for money for a dowry, among other things! She could not picture Olaf doing that! She could imagine him laughing and flinging his arms and legs in the air, or blowing a flickering flame into the air, if anyone even suggested such a thing. Just knowing that someone like Olaf existed gave Sally a light, free feeling in her head.

One effect it had was that she stopped, for the first time since she came home, fretting about Maura and Manus and whether they liked her or not. She had continued to see Maura occasionally. In spite of her uneasiness with Mrs McLoughlin, Sally called up to their house and sat and admired Maura's new clothes, or went for short walks with her in the evenings. Once or twice they had sat together and Maura had showed Sally how to crochet a handkerchief. Even though there was a strain in the friendship, since Sally never felt she could openly talk about what she was feeling with Maura, and since she still found that Maura was over-anxious to impress her, they managed to be companionable. Maura did not have many friends in the neighbourhood: a lot of the girls of her and Sally's age had left home by now, and worked, just as Sally had, as servants in distant places, or had gone to Scotland or America for good. Maura's closest friend, apparently, was somebody called Elizabeth Gallagher, who had gone to stay with her aunt in a village about ten miles away soon after Christmas, and whom she had not seen since then, and, of course, Eileen Carr. But she did not see much of Eileen Carr, either.

Sally had not seen Manus at all in the three weeks since coming home. She found out plenty about him, though, from Maura, who talked about her brother a great deal. He had always been something of a hero in her eyes, and this elevated status had increased as they both grew older. In a way, Maura's endless chatter about Manus upset Sally. It was very hard to have to listen to her describing the events of his life in intimate detail, as if he were a person who had never had anything to do with Sally, a person who would interest her in the way a famous public personage, or a character in a book, might. But not as a boy who had been her friend for almost two years, on and off. But, even though Sally was hurt by Maura's pretended forgetfulness – she was sure it was pretended, although she did not quite understand why – she liked to receive information about Manus, where he was and what he was doing.

After her encounter with the Icelander, she was able to put all her uncomfortable thoughts about Manus out of her head, quite suddenly and miraculously. She was suddenly able to concentrate fully on everything else that was going on in her life. Her mother was still dyeing wool, and she had many other tasks to perform. She milked, she churned, she cleaned the house, she weeded the turnips, the cabbage patch, and the potatoes. She was busy and now, finally, happy as well.

Then Manus came to see her.

He did not come at night when everyone was at home. Indeed he did not come into the house at all. Sally was going up the road to take the cow home in the evening when she encountered him. He was walking along the bit of road beside her house.

"Hello," he said. "I was hoping I'd meet you. I've been waiting for about an hour."

"Hello, Manus," said Sally. Her knees were suddenly shaking so much that she thought she would not be able to go on standing. "You should have come to the house. I was there."

Manus did not respond to this comment.

"Where are you going now?" he asked. "Can I come with you?"

"I'm going to get the cow," said Sally. "You can come if you like."

"Are you going to milk her?"

"Yes, I am," said Sally. "I usually do now. Katie's gone off to work again."

"But you are staying for the summer?"

She nodded.

"I'm glad," he said. "I just found out that you were home a couple of days ago. It's really nice to see you again."

Sally felt a rush of love.

"It's nice to see you too."

They walked along in silence then. From time to time they glanced at one another. His eyes shone and were slightly wet, and Sally too felt tears pricking the backs of her eyes. Walking along with him at her side felt so right, so perfect, that she did not want to say anything. All the anxiety and the angry thoughts she had had about him, all the questions as to why he had not called to see her before now, why he had seemed to be deliberately staying out of her way, vanished completely. They were irrelevant. She knew that he felt what she felt, she believed they were thinking the same thought, as they walked along the little road. The light green and white growth that was all around them and the cooling soft air of the early night were sinking into them. She felt they were part of it all, as much a part of the evening as the long grass that grew beside the spring well where Sally fetched water in a bucket every morning, as much a part of it as the bats that were just beginning to flutter about in the tall trees overhead. She did not feel like a human being, something extra to the world of nature, big and bossy and above it all. She felt like something as small and natural as an insect, or as huge as the ocean, or as light as a feather.

He felt the same way. She knew he did.

He helped her get the cow out of the field – he was better at doing that than Sally was, more competent with animals. Then he walked back with her and the cow, who was called Rose, towards the house.

"I'll call for you tomorrow," he said. "About eight o'clock? We could go for a walk maybe."

"Yes," she said. "Wait for me here, will you?"

"That's what I meant," he said. "Bye."

Sally milked the cow in the green shadows of the byre, leaning her head against the animal's warm flank. She felt as if a mill was grinding happiness out somewhere in the centre of her stomach, and that it was flowing rapidly all through her body. She milked too fast, and upset Rose. She had to force herself to slow down to the normal pace. Her head was light, giddy with this delight that was being created inside of her. As soon as the milk pail was full, she set it down in the back kitchen, and then she ran out into the cooling evening and ran all the way from the house to the shore and back again. And then she went for a walk. When she came in her mother and Packy Doherty and

Madge were still in the kitchen, sitting by the fire, talking.

"You look red, Sally," said her mother. "What have you been doing?"

"Just walking about," she answered.

"Come up to the fire, *a thaisce*, and have a cup of tea."

"No thanks, not tonight. I think I'll just go to bed now. I feel tired for some reason."

Sally couldn't bear the thought of having to sit still, and talk about the weather and how the oats were doing with these old people. She went into the little cool room that she shared now with Janey, who was asleep, a small hot lump under the quilt. She slid in beside her and was grateful for the warmth and the rhythm of her deeply breathing body. But she could not close her eyes or sleep at all that night. She lay with her eyes open. Manus's face hovered somewhere around her head, shimmering through her brain like a lovely reflection in a rippling pond. When she finally fell asleep she dreamed of him. He was travelling with her in a train, through a landscape that she had never seen before. Very bright green pastures rolled away from the sides of the railway track, and a wide blue river flowed under stone bridges. Not far away was a small town, with two steeples rising above it. Manus and she stood together in a corridor linking two carriages. He was towering over her, although in reality she and Manus were about the same height. He was smiling at her and patting her shoulder gently. She felt perfectly calm and perfectly happy.

Then the train stopped at a station, the station in the little town. Sally was no longer in the corridor, she was in a compartment along with an old lady and an elderly gentleman, both heavily dressed in black although the season seemed to be spring or summer. The gentleman was smoking a cigar and the lady had a little dog on her lap to whom she talked all the time. The dog barked, there was a sense of clutter, of food and drink being taken, of smoke, in the compartment. Sally sat pressed against her seat and waited for Manus to return. But she knew he was not coming back. She could see him, in her mind, stepping off the train, not at the station but while the train was in motion. He was dressed in his best suit, a black suit with a white shirt, and wearing his Sunday cap. He stepped off the train into a field as if he were stepping onto a platform, and she knew he would not be back. In the dream this did not concern her at all. The feeling of calm and happiness that she had had in the earlier part continued, even though Manus did not return and even though she had no reason, it seemed, to be anything but alarmed.

8

Sally in Love

Sally felt uneasy when she awoke from this dream. It
was very early in the morning – she had slept for less
than three hours. The first milky grey light was just
beginning to seep into the room. Janey was still asleep,
warm as toast beside her. Sally opened her eyes slowly and
then closed them again. She went over all the details of the
dream in her mind. When she had done that, she felt better
about it, and her concern about its strange ending vanished.
She did not know what it meant, especially as the feeling
she had in the dream was at odds with what happened in it.

She sat up slowly, got out of bed and walked over to
the small window set deep in the wall. She pushed aside
the candle that stood in a saucer on the window-sill, and
stared out. The farmyard was empty. The red roof of the
byre was deep in the shadow of the sycamore trees.
Beyond stretched the oatfield and the cornfield, pools of
pale light, and beyond that the lough. The sun was rising
over the mountains on the other side of the lough, and the
water was black and fiery gold.

Sally looked out, not thinking anything at all.

Then the cock crowed. The morning was filled with his boisterous trumpeting. Her trance, if that's what it was, was broken.

She stretched, smiled and started to put on her clothes. It was too early to get up, but she could not stay in bed any longer. She was full of energy. She felt the day was stretching out before her like a beautiful balmy lake. She wanted to plunge into it and live it without losing one more minute.

When she went into the kitchen she was surprised to find that Granny was awake, puffing on her pipe and saying prayers in a loud hum.

"Who's that?" the old woman asked, when Sally bounded in.

"Good morning, Granny. It's only me, Sally. Would you like something? Can I get you some breakfast?"

"You're up early this morning. Nobody gets up early in this house. All lazy as sin. Early to bed and early to rise makes a man healthy wealthy and wise."

Sally took no notice of Granny, who no longer expected anyone to respond to her running commentary on the ills of humanity, and on the faults of the Gallaghers in particular. If they did she never seemed to hear what their responses were anyway. She stopped talking and said the Rosary instead.

Sally caught the bucket and skipped off to the well. She filled three or four buckets with the clear water, so that they would have a supply lasting most of the day. Then she tidied up the kitchen, set the table, raked out the fire and got it going, and boiled water for tea. The whole house was spick and span by the time her mother got up, bringing Janey with her, at eight o'clock.

"Goodness, what's come over you?" she said. "You must

be getting cracked in your old age."

"Just felt like getting up early today," said Sally. "It's such a good day. It's such a great summer. I love this weather. I love the sunshine. I feel wonderful, all the time."

"I'm glad to hear that, *a thaisce*," said her mother. "We've plenty to do today, as well. It's tomorrow that Miss Bannister is coming, isn't it?"

"The first of July. Yes. That's when she's coming. And today is your last day at school, Janey. Tomorrow you'll be on your holidays, isn't it great?"

"Yes," said Janey. "I hate school."

The day passed in a hectic round of washing, scrubbing, cleaning, cooking, and in general preparing for that completely unprecedented event: the arrival of a paying guest in the Gallagher household. Miss Bannister was coming to stay in Glenbra and learn Irish. A few people had occasionally done this in the past few summers in Glenbra, but this year several more were coming. The McLoughlins were going to have a guest, and some other houses were getting them as well. The people of Glenbra were at first surprised by this sudden display of interest in their home and their language. They had always been taught to consider Glenbra much inferior to the far off places, like Dublin and Belfast, from which these visitors were coming. According to what they knew also, English was a much better and more desirable language than the language they spoke themselves at home, Irish. But now, apparently, this was changing. Glenbra was a popular place, popular enough for people to come and spend their holidays in it. And Irish was something people from Dublin and Belfast and England actually wanted to learn. Oh well, the people shrugged. *Is aisteach an mac é an tsaol!* The wheel of fortune turns, sometimes up and sometimes down. And they said other things, of the same nature. The people of Glenbra were seldom short of a proverb to suit any occasion.

Sally worked harder for her mother on that day than she ever had in her life before, and by evening the house was looking neater and cleaner than she could have imagined possible. It was always neat and clean enough, anyway, but now it absolutely sparkled so much that you felt worried about even walking in it.

At eight o'clock, Mrs Gallagher was still flustering around, getting things even more squared up. Sally threw in her dusters and changed from her old working dress into her Sunday outfit, and said: "I'm going for a walk now. I'll be back soon enough."

She was relieved that her mother did not ask her where she was off to. It was lucky,' she reflected, that she had so often this summer gone on long walks alone in the evening, or gone to talk to Maura. She was not sure whether her mother would allow her to go out like this with Manus or not, but it was easier not to put it to the test.

That evening was one of those which stayed in Sally's memory. Forever afterwards she could replay it in her mind, like a movie – not the black and white ones that were just then becoming available in America, but the coloured film of dreams and memories.

There she is in her mind's eye, a tall girl with a twist of black hair pinned to the back of her head, wearing a white cotton dress with a blue ribbon at the waist, small black boots, polished till they gleamed and worn in honour of Manus. In the white dress her skin, tanned by the sun of this hot summer, looks very brown and healthy, and her eyes gleam. She walks slowly, dwarfed by the huge, spreading sycamores, the leaves of which are big and darkening now, as the summer moves on. She moves away from the house, to where their own street opens onto the laneway, and then walks more slowly towards the place where Manus has said he will meet her. She has looked forward all day to this moment, she is savouring it now and making it last as long as possible. But she is feeling a bit nervous. It's not that she is worried that he will not come. It does not occur to her for one moment that such a thing could happen. She is nervous because the moment she had thought about all day, lived through in a daydream since this time last night, is now going to actually happen. She is not used to this sudden meeting of dreams with reality.

Manus is sitting under the oak tree, clasping his knees. His skin is not tanned: he has been indoors all summer and he has a fair complexion. His hair is a light golden brown, curling around his face. He is wearing some sort of dark coloured trousers and a white shirt, opened at the collar and with the sleeves rolled up.

As soon as she sees him sitting there, all Sally's trepidation, her sense of wonder, her longing and giddy excitement, ease out into that feeling of calmness she had in the dream. A calm natural feeling that everything is just as it should be takes over. This is the feeling she will always have when she is with Manus.

Manus turns to her and stands up, smiling.

"Hello!"

"Hello, Manus. How are you?"

"You look lovely."

"Oh . . . " Sally looks at the ground in embarrassment. But she feels pleased.

"Where will we go?"

"Oh, I don't know," says Sally. When she thinks about where they could go, all the lanes and boreens of Glenbra jumble together in her head like a skein of wool the cat got at. She can't for the life of her imagine where they should go.

"Let's go down to the beach. Would you like that?"

"Oh yes," says Sally. Anywhere will do.

They walk along, keeping a space of about a yard between them.

"You must tell me all about yourself. What has been happening, since I saw you last?"

He had last seen her, last night excepted, and danced with her all night at a party in Elizabeth Gallagher's kitchen six months ago. A great deal has happened since then. Sally does not know where to start.

"Well, I've been in Tyrone, as you know, with the Stewarts, the family I was with before . . . "

"Yes. Tell me their names. I forget what they were called. What was Mrs Stewart called?"

"Her name was Clarissa, and his name is William, and the children . . . "

And so she goes on. Manus asks questions and draws the whole story out of her. He is mightily inquisitive, and wants to know everything about the Stewart house: what sort of fire they had, and what colour the kitchen was, and whether there was a carpet on the parlour floor, and did they have a brass pot with a green plant in it. He wants to know what they ate for breakfast, and how many horses they had, and how many cows, and what work Sally had done for them. He asks so many questions that she has no difficulty at all in chattering on and on, and in turning all the little events of her life over the past year into a colourful and exciting story. Colourful, because he asks for all the detail, and exciting because he seems to be deeply interested in everything she has to say. It is as if every single little thing that had ever happened to her, everything she has seen and heard or even thought, is of the greatest interest. Sally has never known anyone who was as interested in knowing all about this kind of thing. Most people, she feels, would be bored after a few sentences. They might make a pretence of being interested but then stop listening. Not so Manus. Sally is not normally a talkative person, but finds that she can go on like this endlessly.

She is so wrapped up in the pleasure of talking to Manus that she does not have much opportunity for her usual habit of observance. It is quite the opposite experience of talking with Maura: since she nattered on so continually there was usually nothing for Sally to do except watch her, size her up, and criticise her. With Manus the shoe is on the other foot. He is the one who is watching, not critically, but admiringly. He asks his endless stream of questions, and glances happily and encouraging at Sally. She feels very special.

They are walking along a narrow shaded lane beside the hazel wood. The lane is shadowy, overhung with elderflower and brambles. Occasionally they hear the rasp of the corncrake. Occasionally tiny bats, all but invisible, flutter across the road above their heads. Sometimes a dog barks or snaps at them. Then Manus snarls at the dog and kicks him, while at the same time clasping Sally's arm protectively. She knows all these dogs very well, and is well able to deal with them herself, thanks to years of experience, but she is happy to let Manus look after her in this way.

They come to the beach. First they have to cross a river that flows into the sea at that point. There is a line of stepping stones across the river, which is so low by now, owing to the lack of rain, that you can almost walk across on the river bed itself. Sally has always enjoyed stepping from stone to stone, however, taking care not to slip on the slippery stones, taking care not to fall in. When she was a little girl it was a big adventure, the space between the stones vast. Now she can step from one to the other easily, without even exerting herself, but it is fun nevertheless. As they cross the river, Manus takes her hand to help her and when they reach the other side he does not let go. They walk along the river bank, where the grass is very lush and green, until it peters out into sand. Then they begin to walk by the edge of the sea.

There is nobody on the beach. The tide is going out, exposing sweeps of reddish gold sand. It is the same colour as Manus's hair, in fact. Sally thinks this but does not tell it to him. They are both silent now, as they walk hand in hand towards the high cliff, overgrown with greenery, at the far side of the beach. Sally wonders if he plans to climb up that cliff: a narrow path, called "The Seven Bends", winds through the undergrowth until it emerges at the top where a coastguard station, an enormous grey building, stands. She does not want to talk now, though. Holding Manus's hand gives her enough to concentrate on. He feels the same about hers. Neither of them is thinking about anything very much. Their eyes rest on the darkening sea, the wine-tinted sky. The sound of the waves breaking against the sand reaches their ears . . . But in fact they see and hear very little. They are so conscious of being together, that everything else in the world is blotted out.

Sally stumbles over something and falls on the sand. The spell is broken.

"Are you all right?" Manus is all concern. He stoops over her, looks anxiously at her eyes. It was a small fall, really, and the sand is not a dangerous place to land. Tenderly he helps her to her feet.

"I'm fine," says Sally, dusting sand off her clothes. "What is that?"

"What?"

"What I tripped over."

He stoops down. There is a little tussock of sand at his feet. He scrapes away some of it and finds underneath a large, pear-shaped bottle. It was a wine bottle, Sally learned later, but she did not know that then. Neither she nor Manus had ever seen a bottle of wine, except for altar wine in the sacristy at the church – Manus would have seen that. He was an altar boy when younger.

Manus takes up the bottle and shakes off the sand. It is a corked bottle: the neck is firmly stopped with a cork which he tries to remove, but cannot.

"Damn it," he says. "It won't come out."

"Oh well," says Sally, who is a little disappointed that their walk has been transformed by the discovery of this bottle, "maybe you should take it home and open it there?"

"No," says Manus, setting his mouth in the stubborn way which Sally recognises as being typical of a boy or a man determined to do something, no matter how idiotic. "I'm going to open it here."

He starts searching around in the shells and stones for something. He picks up a sharp stone and tries to prise off the cork with that. It doesn't work, of course. Sally looks on impatiently. She knows that nothing they can find on this beach is going to uncork the bottle. And what will they find inside anyway? Nothing, is most likely the answer.

Manus fiddles with the sharp stone and the cork for ages. Sally begins to walk, irritably, up and down at the edge of the waves. She hears a crack: smashed glass. Manus has broken the bottle against a rock. She sees him standing there, with the big, jagged-edged bottle in one hand and a piece of paper in the other.

"Look!" he says. "A message. There's a message in the bottle!"

Sally rushes over to see what the message is.

She reads:

"Ocean Current Report. Division of Marine Meteorology of the United States. Hydrographic Office. Thrown overboard 25.23n, 26.53w. Signed John Douglas, 3rd Officer."

"What does it mean?" she asks Manus.

"I don't know," he says.

"Maybe it is someone who needs to be rescued from cannibals!" says Sally.

"Maybe it's a clue to hidden treasure!" says Manus.

"What will we do with it?" Sally asks.

"I don't know yet," Manus sounds more serious now. "I'll think about it."

He takes her hand and they turn back towards the river.

9

The Visitor

The next day the Visitor arrived.

Mrs Gallagher was up very early in the morning, making last minute preparations and making everybody feel uncomfortable. Granny got more and more irritable and expressed her irritation by spitting tobacco stained blobs onto the floor which Mrs Gallagher had been carefully cleaning for days.

"If you don't stop that I'll kill you!" screamed Mrs Gallagher, when she had done this about four times.

Janey started to cry then. It was unheard of for her mother to become so angry. Sally picked her up and brought her down to the beach, to have a little dip. Sally seldom got into the water herself: big girls didn't. But Janey was still allowed to splash around and she enjoyed that very much.

The Visitor came at four o'clock in the evening. By that time, Granny, Sally and Janey wished they had never heard tell of her, and Mrs Gallagher was so jittery that there was no point in even trying to talk to her.

The Visitor – everyone, even Janey, knew that her name

was Miss Bannister, but they referred to her only as "The Visitor", and always would – arrived in a pony and trap. The Gallaghers were all in the kitchen, poised for welcome, when they heard the clip-clop of the pony's hooves on the cobblestones. The three mobile Gallaghers immediately jumped up and ran out into the street, while Granny pulled back her bed curtain, stuck out her head, and lay ready to ambush the Visitor as soon as she came through the kitchen door.

The Visitor was a small dark-haired woman, aged about thirty, Sally thought. She was wearing a dark blue jacket, a white blouse and a straw hat. The rest of her was covered with a plaid rug while she was sitting in the trap. When she stepped down, you could see that she had a dark blue skirt, matching the jacket, and black boots.

Her face was very pale and looked sad and tired. But when she saw the Gallaghers, lined up on the doorstep in their white summer dresses, she broke into a smile and suddenly looked mischievous and light-hearted.

"Hello, hello!" she said, in a high-pitched, thin voice. "Hello, hello!"

The driver helped her down from the trap and she walked quickly up to Mrs Gallagher and shook hands with her.

"How are you?" asked Mrs Gallagher. "You must be very tired after your journey."

"Pardon?" said the Visitor, in her surprised, high voice.

The Gallaghers understood from this that she had a good bit to learn, in the way of Irish. If she did not understand "How are you?" she did not know much. Sally and Mrs Gallagher understood also that, instead of speaking Irish, they would have to speak English to the Visitor. Otherwise they would not be able to communicate at all. But in the letter they had received from the Visitor she had given strict instructions that only Irish was to be spoken while she was staying in the house.

It was not easy.

Sally tried again, speaking slowly this time.

"Are . . . you . . . tired?"

"Pardon?" said the Visitor, looking a bit cross. "Oh yes, the Gaelic. Of course you are speaking the Gaelic. I think I am too tired to learn any today. I'll start tomorrow. Oh, don't tell me that none of you can speak English? But of course you don't, you are true native Irish speakers . . . monoglots . . . charming, really . . . "

Sally broke in here.

"Oh no," she said, in English. "We all speak. All speak English here."

The Visitor smiled in relief.

"Well, I am glad to hear that! Of course, of course, of course, my ambition is to be a fluent Gaelic speaker by the time I leave here. I am determined as to that. But just for the moment . . . it has been a long day, you know, a long day and a long journey. I simply do not have the energy for foreign languages at the moment."

"Please come in," said Sally.

They trooped inside.

"Oh, how delightful it all is!" said the Visitor, sitting down on the best chair, as was only right. "How quaint and charming! I do declare, I have never been in such a pretty little house. There is nothing better than the genuine peasant culture, that is what I always say, so much more beautiful, so much more primary, than anything urbanisation can produce. May I have some tea and a slice of bread and butter if you please? I never have anything but bread and butter with my tea."

"We have a raisin scone, would you like that?"

"Oh, a raisin *sconn*! It sounds irresistible. The true Irish home baking. I think that just this once I will break my rule and have raisin scone, yes I do think so. It may be the death of me, I suffer from the cruellest indigestion, you know, if I step out of line at all, but after all it is the first day of my vacation, yes I will have some raisin scone. And some plain bread and butter. You make all your own bread I suppose?"

"Oh yes."

"So much better than anything you can buy in the shop. I would love to make my own bread but of course I never can, I am so frightfully busy all the time. My job is outrageously demanding, no one can ever believe what pains schoolteachers go to, they think it is an easy job, but, my dear, nothing could be further from the truth, it is the most demanding and tiring job in the world. At the end of each term I am totally exhausted. And term finished just four days ago, I can hardly believe it. Already I am here."

"How was your journey?" asked Sally, slightly nervous at the thought of the tirade that this question might bring.

"My journey was long, so terribly long, that is the principal thing that I remember about it at this point. But apart from that it was quite comfortable. You know I live in Bray in County Wicklow? I took the train to Dublin. And then the train from Dublin to Strabane, and from there I have travelled by a stage coach and then a pony and trap. But it has all been absolutely delightful. I have seen so much and the weather has been so heavenly. I was prepared for heavy rain. I was warned you know by everyone who'd ever been here that it rained all the time in Donegal. "Wonderful place, Gee!" they said, "but it never stops pouring. Bring your sou'wester, bring your gumboots, bring your galoshes, bring all the rubber wear you have in your wardrobe. Leave behind your muslins and straw hats, you will not need them!"

"We are having a drought," said Sally. "We are afraid the crops will burn in the fields."

"Oh dear yes, isn't it terrible? I saw some fields of the darkest most golden corn, it looked like something you might see in Tuscany, it reminded me of my holiday there last year. So beautiful. And to think that now it is like that here as well, well, I do declare . . . "

"Will you sit down at the table, ma'm, and have your tay now?" said Mrs Gallagher. Janey stared at the Visitor, wondering if she were likely to have a present in her bag.

"Who in the name of God is that creature?" Granny's voice suddenly emerged from the recess, quavering and crackling across the room. The Visitor looked startled, but luckily did not understand. Granny spoke no English.

"She's an Irish scholar, Granny," Sally explained. "She's staying with us for a month, to learn Irish."

Granny laughed.

"Glory be to God," she cackled, "did you ever hear the like of that! And what sort of a one is she anyway? She looks like a Protestant sort of a one to me. Where does she come from at all?"

"She is from Dublin, Granny, from outside Dublin. Maybe she is Protestant, I haven't asked her."

"That's my grandmother," Sally turned, and explained to the Visitor. "She is very old and she stays in that bed there all the time."

"How fascinating!" said the Visitor. "I have heard of this. It's called the bed outshot, is it not?"

"We always call it Granny's bed," said Sally.

"May I take a peep?" the Visitor was already over at Granny's bed, pulling at the curtains and taking a good look at Granny. Granny had been spruced up for the occasion, of course, just like everyone and everything else in the house. Mrs Gallagher had washed her face and her hair, and put on a clean shift. She looked very nice resting on her white pillow, with her silver hair neatly combed and wrapped around her head, and her black shawl over her shoulders. Her shift was snow white, and, for once, she was not smoking. The pipe lay hidden under the pillow, where she always kept it when she was not using it, with a small supply of tobacco.

"Hello!" said the Visitor. She took Granny's frail white hand in hers. "It is such a pleasure to meet you. I hope we become good friends."

"Long life to you," said Granny, in Irish. "Young woman, whoever you are. That's a nice hat she has on her," she said to Sally. "You should have a hat like that yourself. Ask her to give it to you."

"What did she say?" the Visitor asked.

"She said she wishes you well. She likes your hat, too."

"Oh goodness, how sweet of her to say so. Tell her I like her shawl, and her bed, and the house, and all of you. Tell her I like everything and that I know in my bones that I am going to be very happy here."

Sally told her grandmother an edited version of this, and then, to her relief, the Visitor moved over to the table and began to talk about food, crockery, cutlery, meals she had eaten in other places, and the price of bread.

Sally had another visitor that evening, a surprise visitor: Maura. It was very unusual for her to walk over to the Gallaghers' in this way, and when Sally saw her she felt alarmed. She was sure the visit had something to do with Manus.

Maura came into the kitchen, something she had not done in years. She was all dressed up, in a navy and white dress, white stockings, her button shoes. She even had gloves. She sat down and had some tea and was introduced to the Visitor, who was only too glad to make the acquaintance of another Glenbra native.

"I hope you like it here," said Maura. "We have someone staying at our house, too. A Mr Curtis. He is a professor in Trinity College, you know, and he has stayed with us before. He is not one of the new visitors. He says he is more at home with us than in his own home in Dublin."

"How charming of him. Learned people always like the simple way of life, I know. My dear cousin Roger likes nothing better than to muck in with positive savages, you know, in the jungles of Africa and such places. And he is very fond of Donegal too. I wish he would come here. It would be a wonderful experience for him, and it would be a splendid experience for all of you to see him."

"I'm sure it would," simpered Maura, who did not know who she was talking about. "Perhaps you can bring him up to our house for tea some afternoon? Mother thought you might like to meet Professor Curtis."

"Oh that would be wonderful. We would love it. Now who is this professor? Is he involved with the Gaelic League in Dublin? I would have heard of him probably if he had been."

"Oh yes I think he is a member of that," said Maura.

"Well he could not be a member. It hasn't been established yet. It is still a twinkle in someone's eye, so to speak. My friend Ada Mac Neill has been telling me about it. Her father is organising it, they will inaugurate it any day now."

"What is it?" asked Sally, to cover the slight confusion that followed this exchange.

"It will be a society to promote Irish language and culture, you know, to restore to Ireland its true heritage, so long derided by the conqueror. They will hold night classes in Irish and organise other cultural activities, I don't know what exactly. It will be very important. It is, they say, the most important thing to happen in Ireland in centuries."

"Learning Irish is becoming something a lot of people like to do now," Sally half said, half asked.

"Of course. All intelligent people would want to do that. And eventually all of them will. Now then, I must go to bed. I need my rest if I am to set off on the right foot tomorrow. Goodnight to you all."

The Visitor went to bed.

Maura began to pout. She took her gloves from the table and began to pull them back on.

"Are you off so soon, Maura?" Sally asked.

"Yes. I really must go. Daddy is taking me and Manus to visit Eileen Carr, in the horse and car."

"Manus? But I am meeting Manus tonight."

Sally blurted this out before she had a chance to think of what she was saying.

"You? Meeting Manus? Really?" Maura laughed, and looked disdainfully at Sally from the top of her head to the toes of her feet. "So how long has this been going on?" she asked, in a small cold voice.

"Me meeting Manus? We've always been friends, you know that."

"Hmm," said Maura. "I wasn't aware of it I must admit." She gave a dry little laugh. "The best of luck to you!"

She didn't look as if she meant it. Her face was white, her eyes chilly as ice. She could hardly get the words out of her mouth. Dislike of Sally was choking her. Sally looked at her in alarm. She had guessed that Maura did not like her as much as before, and bore some sort of resentment towards her. But Maura had kept that more or less buried inside her, and Sally had chosen to ignore it and hope that it would all go away. But it had not gone away. And now here it was, a surge of pure hostility – jealousy, anger, hatred, whatever it was – delivered like a blow in her face, or like a venomous spit. Sally did not know how to cope with it. She was glad that Maura gave up, and simply left the house.

10

Eviction

*T*he Visitor had gone to bed, and so had Janey. Mrs
Gallagher was in the kitchen, waiting for Packy
Doherty to call. Granny was sitting up in bed, saying her
evening Rosary.

Sally slipped out, saying quickly "I'll be back soon," to
forestall any objections.

Manus was under the oak tree.

Sally ran up to him. He held his arms out and she
leaped into them.

She stayed in his arms for at least five minutes. It was
such a comforting place to be, cradled against his big warm
chest. Sally thought she could stay there forever.

But after a while – at the same moment – they pulled
away from each other. Manus laughed.

"Hello!" said Sally.

He laughed again, pulled her hair, and said "Hello
yourself."

They began to walk towards the beach. This was to be
the walk they always took whenever they were together
that summer. For ever afterwards Sally would associate that

particular mile of laneway, with its spicy brambles and its green hazelnuts with love and with Manus.

He was quieter tonight and less inquisitive. He had had a busy day at the store, which had included some problems, but he would not tell Sally what they were.

"Have you solved the mystery of the message in the bottle?"

"The what?"

"You know, the bottle we found the other night."

"I'd forgotten all about it."

Sally found this faintly disgruntling.

"Maybe you should ask your professor?"

"Professor?"

"The fellow who is staying at your house, learning Irish and so on."

"Oh, him. Is he a professor? He's not there yet anyway. At the house, he is coming tomorrow. How do you know about him?"

"Your sister told me."

"You've been talking to Maura today, then?"

"Yes. She came down to our place, to take a look at our visitor, I think, mainly. Then she told me about yours. And, Manus?"

"Yes?"

"I told her about us. That I was meeting you. Walking out with you. She wasn't too pleased."

"No. You probably shouldn't have done that."

"She has to find out sometime. I don't understand why she is so upset about it anyway. Do you?"

"Hm?" Manus seemed to be lost in thought. "Oh, no, I have no idea." He smiled and said briskly: "Now, tell me all about your visitor."

It was quite late when Sally came home. She and Manus spent a very long time saying goodbye. Sally found it almost impossible to break away from him even though she knew he would be there again tomorrow. She could not understand why parting from him was so hard: she had never felt like this saying goodbye to anyone else, not since she was a tiny little girl saying goodbye to her mother when she first set off to school. Or saying goodbye to her father when he went off on long fishing trips. It was like that, like being a little child illogically afraid of being abandoned. The only way she could tear herself away was by closing her eyes and pretending she was going to do something really frightening and dangerous requiring enormous courage, like diving into an icy pool from a great high cliff. "Goodnight!" she'd say, with her eyes closed, and then she'd walk away very quickly without looking back. And Manus would look after her and scratch his head.

As soon as she did it and was safely separated from him it did not feel so bad. She could have kicked herself for making such heavy weather of it, but every night it was just the same.

When she came in, her mother, Madge, and Packy Doherty were at the fire. Packy was eating a bowl of yellow meal: he was such a familiar presence that he was treated like one of the family already, Sally thought, grimacing. Katie was probably right, although she couldn't imagine how her mother could bear the thought of being married to such a boring old man.

All three were looking a bit morose tonight, their faces sad in the flickering firelight.

"An eviction notice has been served on Bridgie Greene," her mother explained. "She's to leave tomorrow if she can't pay her rent. She hasn't paid any for close on two years, and the landlord can't wait any longer."

"Aye," said Madge glumly. "And she's not the only one. There's four or five notices gone out."

"I thought things were supposed to be getting better now, with the Land League and everything."

"Some of them won't pay the rent out of badness, because they think it's too high. They're holding it back to force the landlords to lower it or to being shame on them by making them have evictions."

"Aye, and then there's the like of Bridgie who hasn't the money for any rent no matter how low it is." Packy spoke the longest sentence she'd ever heard him utter. "The land acts helped some people who had something already, enough together to make a start at buying out their places. But they're no help to people like Bridgie. Poor Bridgie, may God and His Blessed Mother pity her, and her with the six weans. What is she going to do at all?"

"Won't she get some kind of a hut to live in even if she is put out?"

"She will. A mean little wooden hut that Bridgie won't like and that the weans won't fit into."

"It's better than nothing."

"It is, God help us," said Mrs Gallagher. "What time is the eviction on at?"

"Och, the constabulary will be around first thing. They've issued two notices and yesterday she got the final writ. It's all happening tomorrow. Are you going?"

"It might be interesting for yon Visitor to go around and see what goes on."

"What goes on in this part of the world, Gaelic Ireland, you mean."

Manus had given her the phrase "Gaelic Ireland". He

was clever about knowing things like that. He had a way with words, Manus, and all the most up to the minute turns of phrase and expressions. He read the newspaper, *The Donegal Independent*, at the shop. Sometimes he told Sally jokes he read in it.

"Yes, maybe you'll go along with her Sally, to keep her company. You've never seen an eviction yourself, have you?"

"No."

"You might as well go then. You can always give Bridgie a hand with her things, she'll need help to move her bits and pieces into the new hut. Those children of hers are not much good for anything. Sure the youngest is only three or four. And the three big ones are away in Argyll tatie hoking."

"I'll go, I'll go."

Sally had anxious feelings about the eviction. Would it be so brutal and shocking that she would not be able to contain herself, but would burst into tears in public, or scream and roar? She imagined Bridgie being picked up and flung headlong into the ditch by a police constable. That's what happened, they said: "she was thrown out onto the side of the road."

But when she and the Visitor arrived at Bridgie's cottage, the eviction turned out to be an efficient, highly organised affair, like an auction or a circus or some sort of public entertainment. It was already well underway.

Hundreds of people were involved, many more than you would imagine necessary simply to get a poor widow and three small children to leave their home. There was Mr Borland, the landlord's agent, a burly man in a tweed jacket and thick jodhpurs, jigging around on a big fat horse, looking very important. There were a few other men from the landlord's demesne, on foot, carrying sticks. In addition there were about five policemen on horseback, and five others on foot.

Besides these, there were dozens of onlookers, a young man in a green coat carrying a notebook into which he pencilled notes furiously, a few people who looked a bit like the Visitor and were obviously other Irish students like her, and two photographers, one stationed at each corner of the yard in front of the house.

"Good gracious, I hadn't expected to find such a large crowd!" exclaimed the Visitor, who was wearing a solemn face, as befitted a sad occasion. "Quite a shindig, isn't it! There's a reporter – I must talk to him. And one would not have expected photographers. I wonder who they are?"

One of the photographers, a tall man with a long grey beard, was standing behind his camera. The other was busy taking a photograph, crouching over the big wooden camera. The Visitor went up to the man who was disengaged.

"Hello, my good fellow," she said, assuming, correctly, that a photographer would be an English speaker. "Would you mind telling me who you and your colleague are?"

"I'll be happy to introduce myself, ma'am," the man said, bowing slightly. "Robert French, photographer to Lawrence Studios, Dublin. My colleague . . . " he waved airily in his direction " . . . is from Londonderry. His name escapes me at the moment."

"My name is Geraldina Bannister," said the Visitor. "I am here on a cultural visit, as you might say. Do you often photograph scenes such as this?"

"We have been doing some evictions of late, yes. Part of our Irish Life Series, you know. Evictions, The Donegal

Cloak, The Galway Cloak, and Irish Jaunting Car. That sort of thing. Usually I do not concern myself with minor evictions such as this, but I was in the area photographing scenery and I heard it was on. It's quite a good one, actually. Sad, of course, for the family. But from my point of view ideal, with the young children and so on. The woman is quite photogenic, even in those rags, isn't she?"

Sally and the Visitor looked dutifully at Bridgie, who was sitting surrounded by the children on a patch of ground at the side of the cottage. She was a big, dark woman with strong features and bright black eyes. Dressed all in black – raggedy black skirt, black shawl – with her bony feet and strong hands, she could be said to look striking. Sally had never thought of it before.

Suddenly Robert French started to wave his hands in the air and to exclaim excitedly: "Look! Look! Here they come with the battering ram. I'm afraid you must excuse me now, ladies. I have to go to work."

By now, Bridgie's furniture and other belongings were out on the roadside: she was sitting on a kitchen chair, with all her pots and pans, her bed, her clothes, in short, the entire contents of her house, at her feet. Her little girls were playing with the cups and saucers, having a pretend tea party. Dónal, the little boy, was crawling around getting under everybody's feet. Nobody was making any attempt to move any of the furniture yet, although a makeshift hut had been erected for Bridgie during the past few days. Everyone was waiting to see what would happen next.

The battering ram was a huge iron pole, which travelled from place to place on a big wooden cart. Six men were now positioning the cart directly in front of the cottage door. Then they slid the battering ram, which was operated on a sort of swivel, off the cart, and moved it towards the door.

"Hold it there for a minute, please!"

It was not a reprieve from the landlord. It was Robert French, the photographer.

"I'd like to get a picture of you just as you move the ram to the door. All right? Just hold it there for two minutes. You'll be immortalised! That's it. Lovely . . . lovely . . . "

The six men, constables in full uniform and some of the landlord's men, stood holding the enormous, heavy battering ram, while Mr French took a photograph. Then, when he had finished, they heaved, pushed the ram forward, and began to ram it into the cottage door.

In a short time the door and part of the wall had been broken down.

"Are we not doing the roof too, lads?" someone shouted.

"The roof, boys, shouldn't we do the roof?"

There seemed to be some confusion as to whether the roof was to be broken or not. It hardly mattered much one way or the other: it was in very bad shape already, an old thatch that hadn't been replaced in years. Half the ropes were rotted away.

Everyone, even Bridgie, looked expectantly at the agent. He looked over the house.

"Leave it," he said.

With that, the constables mounted their horses, the men put the battering ram back onto its cart, and the whole troop trotted away down the road. The onlookers stared after them. As they went, Bridgie stood up. Pulling herself to her full height, which was considerable, she stretched out her arm and pointed after them. In a loud incantatory voice she intoned these words:

"The devil take you, Bernard Borland. You and yours

will rot in your graves before one year is out. With that I curse you from the bottom of my heart."

The agent stopped in his tracks. All the other riders stopped too, and stared at Bridgie, who was now looking very impressive indeed. She loomed larger than life, a long thin black creature with gleaming eyes outlined against the low hills and the strong blue sky. Sally could see Robert French frantically fiddling with his camera, pulling out plates of glass and fitting others in.

But before he managed to set up the camera Bridgie had sat down. Bernard Borland kicked his horse and galloped off. Immediately his men and the constabulary followed suit. The large cavalcade galloped away down the narrow country lane.

Sally looked admiringly at Bridgie.

"She cursed them! Isn't that what she did? She cursed the landlord and his crowd?" The Visitor was also thrilled by what had happened.

"Yes. She is a widow and she believes that her curse has a special power. It's supposed to be especially powerful. They say a widow's curse works," said Sally.

"Isn't that absolutely fascinating. I do hope that it does, don't you?"

"Yes," said Sally. "I suppose I do. It'd be nice to think that she can get revenge in some way or other, all right. And that's probably the only way she has." She sighed. She didn't believe for one minute in the power of the widow's curse, or any other kind of curse. She thought that she must find out what the Irish politicians were doing now to help make life better for people like Bridgie. People like her. Since Parnell had died, nearly two years ago, and the fuss about him had faded away, nothing much seemed to be going on at all. People continued to talk about Home

Rule now and then. Manus had told her that the Orangemen were protesting against it in speeches they made in Ramelton during the 12th of July celebrations. Even the minister in the Presbyterian church there had spoken out against it, saying that Home Rule was Rome Rule.

"See the power the Church had over the population in the Parnell case," he had said. "That's the power they'll have over the Irish government if we get Home Rule." But although the Orangemen were worried about it nobody else seemed to believe Home Rule was close to being a reality. Interest in it seemed to have died with Parnell.

"Listen," said Sally, "I'm going to help her move her goods and chattels now. Maybe you would like to go on home. You'll find your way yourself, won't you?"

"Oh yes, of course I will," said the Visitor. "I am going to go on a good long walk now, before going home for lunch. First, however, I am going to have another word with that nice Mr French. Goodbye, my dear, and thank you so much for bringing me here. It is really an eye-opener. That poor unfortunate woman! Oh dear, oh dear me," and suddenly the Visitor started to weep.

Sally went over to Bridgie.

11

Photographs

*O*thers of Bridgie's neighbours had by now gathered around her and began carrying objects from the roadside towards the temporary shelter which had been built for her. This was about a mile from her own home, a wooden hut that once had been a railway carriage. It was erected on a small triangular patch of scrubby land that lay between the parameters of two estates. No landlord or farmer laid claim to it as his own.

Sally picked up a bundle of clothes and said to Bridgie:

"I'll carry these down for you. Are you coming along yourself now?"

"I may as well," Bridgie no longer looked imperious and powerful as she had when casting her curse on the agent. Now she was completely worn out. There were dark hollows under her eyes and her mouth turned down grimly. She looked like someone who had spent a great deal of time crying.

She took her youngest child, who had long black ringlets and was dressed in a torn white petticoat even though he was a boy, by the hand. The little girls clamoured to take her other hand and continued to squabble about who should hold it even as they all walked slowly along the road.

Sally did not know what she should say to Bridgie. The eviction itself had been such an ostentatious display that she had not felt deeply moved while it was taking place. She could not believe that anyone had, although everyone said, "It's very sad," all the time. It had been unreal, like a play. And Bridgie's own performance in the closing scene had made it more bizarre. Sally had felt uplifted after that as she might feel uplifted after hearing some rousing song. It was as if Bridgie had come through some great battle as the victor.

Now it did not feel like that at all. The curve of Bridgie's shoulders and every line in her body spoke of defeat. The little children, who only half understood what was going on, and looked at Sally and at Bridgie with wide eyes, hopeful of an explanation and a happy ending, made the tragedy completely real.

"It's a good thing we're having a fine summer," said Sally. It sounded pathetic, but she wanted to say something optimistic.

Bridgie did not reply.

"You'll be all right for a few weeks anyway," she continued, desperately. "There are some funds to help you, aren't there, in the Evicted Tenants' Fund? And maybe the Congested Districts Board will give you a house eventually."

"Maybe," Bridgie was sobbing. She did not have much faith in official organisations.

"It's horrible, yes, it is really horrible. Because what are you going to do in the end?"

"God alone knows," said Bridgie. "It's the workhouse

for me, or the road, that's all there is. And the weans will have to go to the workhouse or the orphanage."

At the sound of the word "orphanage" the oldest little girl, who was seven, started to cry. Even she had heard rumours about the orphanage, far away in Ballyshannon. Her mother had sometimes threatened to send her there if she wasn't good. Everyone knew it was the worst place in the world for a child to be. The nuns beat the children with bamboo canes for the slightest reason. They made them get up at five o'clock in the morning and work all day and they never gave them enough to eat, let alone any love or kindness. The nuns were called Sisters of Mercy. "The Sisters of Mercy have no mercy," people said about them, "And the Sisters of Charity have no charity." Life in the orphanage was full of cruelty and misery. Everybody knew that. Even the workhouse, where you got up at 6:30 in the morning and stayed up, scrubbing floors, until 9 o'clock at night, would be better than the orphanage.

Tears came to Sally's eyes too as she thought of it.

"But I won't do it," said Bridgie, her black eyes taking on some of their fierceness. "I won't let that happen to them. I'll die first."

Sally felt a surge of hope like the faintest gleam of yellow light after a terrible storm. Suddenly she realised that Bridgie had power. Her power was not the widow's magic. Her curses were not necessarily going to be efficacious. But in the strength of her will there was power and that in itself was a kind of magic. The question was, would it be strong enough to overcome the disastrous circumstances?

They came to the hut. Perched on its scrubby patch of heather on the side of the hill, directly overlooking the sea, it made Sally want to burst out laughing. Some bright spark had painted it yellow, and it looked crazy and comical like something a clown in a circus would live in. It did not look a bit like a shelter for someone who was on the brink of, or already in, dire poverty, and who was staring total ruin in the face.

The children loved it.

"Mammy mammy!" the little boy said. "Nice new house! Nice new house! Can me go inside?"

He laughed and giggled, tumbling up to the little door of the wooden railway carriage. His mother smiled as she looked at him, and again Sally felt her heart lift. You could see so easily how much Bridgie loved those children.

Sally was met on the road outside her own house by the Visitor.

"Oh Sally, Sally, there you are at last!" she said. "I thought you would never come home. Something wonderful is going to happen to you!"

Sally was still wrapped in thoughts of Bridgie Greene and her family, and found this sudden exuberance irritating. The Visitor behaved more like a child, she thought, than someone who was headmistress of a school. What sort of a school could someone like that be headmistress of? The pupils must run rings around her.

"What is it?" Sally was polite as always.

"Mr French wants to take your picture."

Sally was taken aback.

"Take my picture? Why?"

"Well . . . I asked him to take mine, you know. I would like very much to have my picture taken here in Glenbra, in front of the house and so on. So he has come to do that. And now he would like to take yours too. He asked if he could. You and your mother and he'd like to take your grandmother too but of course that is out of the question. She won't hear of it."

Sally followed the Visitor down the street. Outside the house, among the hens and ducks, Mr French and a boy who turned out to be his assistant were standing, with their camera set up and various bags and bits of equipment on the ground. Mrs Gallagher was sitting outside the door beside the rainwater barrel. She had brought out a kitchen chair and the little spinning wheel which she had got from the Congested Districts Board a year before, for spinning flax – she had not yet used it for this purpose. She had never spun flax before and didn't think it was a good idea to start now. But the wheel worked well for wool, and she had spun wool on it. She had on her best Paisley shawl. Mr French settled the shawl on her shoulder so that it draped artistically and positioned the wheel in such a way that he could get a good view of it.

"That's it," he said. "Hold that pose now."

He scampered back to the camera and took the photograph.

"I'll take it again!" his voice came, muffled, from under the cloak. "Hold it there. Wonderful!"

He took six photographs of Mrs Gallagher. Then he set to work on Sally.

He wanted her to pose as an Irish peasant girl.

"Have you got a woollen skirt?" he asked. "Some more traditional looking clothes than those ones you have on?"

Sally was wearing an old cotton dress that had once belonged to Mrs Stewart. She went inside and changed into her homespun skirt, white blouse and little tweed polky. She hardly ever wore them any more and the polky was tight under the arms. Mr French liked it, though.

"Great!" he said. "Now let down your hair."

Sally unpinned her hair. She hadn't had it cut in ages, since she always put it up, and it flowed down to her waist.

"That is perfect. Now, I want you to sit here beside the creels of turf. You don't have an ass handy, do you?"

"No. Not handy."

"Do you have one at all?"

"We have an ass. He's over in the hill field. It would take half an hour to get him."

Robert French scratched his head and looked anxiously at the sky.

"Will you get it, please?"

"The ass?"

"Yes, yes, the ass."

Sally looked at her mother.

"Run off now and get it when he asks you!" she said, as if there was no reason to question this at all.

Sally tucked her hair behind her ears and headed off for the hill field where their donkey was grazing. She hoped nobody would see her, looking this way, and luckily nobody did.

When she came back, Robert French, the boy, the Visitor and her mother, were sitting outside. They had brought the table out to the street at the Visitor's suggestion – the Gallaghers never dreamed of having a meal outdoors normally. Now they were all seated at it, drinking tea and eating bread and jam. Somebody, Sally could guess who, had placed a bunch of buttercups and camomile daisies in a jam jar on the middle of the table. It all looked very gay.

"Come and join us, Sally! We're eating al fresco!"

"No no," Robert French jumped up. "I must take this picture before the light fades any more. Ah yes, the perfect donkey. Good old Ned. Put the creels on him, will you, like a good girl, and then we'll be ready to go?"

Sally strapped the creels onto the donkey's back, and then they all had to put some turf in the creels so that it would look as if she were just coming down from the hill. Then she had to stand by the ass's head for half an hour, and smile, while Robert French took her picture.

Later that evening, exhilarated by the photography session, perhaps, and frightened by the story of Bridgie Greene's eviction, Mrs Gallagher told Sally that she was going to marry Packy Doherty.

12

Kiss

"*I* don't know how she can do it." Sally was sitting on the boathouse slip with Manus.

"It's not so strange really, is it?" said Manus. "She must be lonely without your father, and it's hard for a woman to manage a place on her own."

Exactly what that fellow from Iceland, Olaf, had said.

"Isn't it terrible that women marry men just because they own a farm or have some money or something?" Sally looked disconsolately out over the shadowy waters of the lough. The seagulls were wheeling in the blue sky, cotton wool clouds gathered over the lilac-coloured hills. It was a fine summer's day again.

"How do you know she doesn't like him? Anyway, men have to marry women for the same sort of reason," said Manus. "You can't afford to marry someone who hasn't any land, or a business, or money. It's a pity, but that's how it is. That's life."

He jumped up and began to throw flat stones into the water, letting them skim along the surface of the sea, hopping sometimes once, sometimes three or four times.

He was highly skilled at this activity and much preferred doing it to talking about marriage, a subject which he found distasteful and embarrassing. Girls were always talking about it, it seemed to him. Even Sally, who was an unusual girl.

Sally stood up so that he would be able to hear what she was saying.

"I want to have a different kind of life from that," she said. "Don't you?"

"Hm? Haven't thought about it really. When is your mother getting married by the way?"

"In October. The banns will be called at Mass next Sunday. October! I mightn't even be here!"

"Where are you going? If you're going into service again it won't be before November, will it? And you won't go into service now, will you? You won't have to if she marries him. You can help them on the farm."

Sally smiled. "Would you like me to stay?"

"Of course I'd like you to stay," said Manus in an impatient voice. He stood looking at the sea for a minute. Then he turned to Sally and put his arms around her. He kissed her, standing on the slip, in the sunshine of a Sunday morning. She closed her eyes and heard the seagulls calling and the waves lapping against the end of the slip.

The first kiss. It happened that suddenly. It felt like the splash of a stone hitting smooth water, or the twittering of birds first thing on a summer's morning. It felt like sunshine, fresh rain, mountain streams. But more magical and more delightful than any of those things. And, in spite of everything that happened afterwards, Sally was always grateful to Manus for doing it, at that time and in that place, and for giving her one perfect memory to carry with her throughout her life.

She had not abandoned Maura completely. After the evening when she had told her about Manus, she had not called on her for about a week. By then, the incident had lost its significance. She could not believe that Maura really hated her all that much, and it seemed silly to let their acquaintanceship end on account of a single falling out. So one evening, when she had not arranged to meet Manus, Sally went over to call on her.

Maura was surprised to see her, and it was clear that she felt some relief. She behaved much more kindly to Sally than she had done all summer.

"Mother's out," was the first thing she said. "Why don't you come in? I've got raspberry cordial from the shop."

She and Sally sat in the kitchen drinking fizzy red lemonade. The room had been freshly whitewashed. There were blue checked curtains on the windows and vases of pink dog roses on the ledges.

"We got it done up for the professor, you know, our visitor," explained Maura. "Mother really loves having him."

"She does?"

"Well, he's company for her, actually. Dad and Manus are never at home and she gets dull with nobody but me. Then she starts to believe she's sick. You should just see all the pills and medicines she's got!"

Maura brought Sally upstairs to her parents' bedroom. On a table beside the bed there were at least twenty tins, boxes and bottles containing various medicines – Brandreth's Sugar-coated Pills, Jacob's Oil for Lumbago, Powell's Balsam of Aniseed.

Sally picked one up. "'Cupiss's Constitution Balls'. What are these for?"

"Oh, she's got everything you could think of!"

"'For Horses, Neat Cattle, Sheep and Calves.' Does your mother need this?"

"Must have got here by mistake. Look, though, she's even got a book. *Medical Matters. By a Lady Doctor.*"

Inside were descriptions of female diseases, their causes, symptoms and cures.

"'Cystitis'," Maura read. "'Inflammation of the bladder area. Caused by infections. Should be treated by drinking copious quantities of water. A patent cream is also available from the address supplied. This should be applied especially before and after marital relations (these may be especially painful initially but with careful attention the worst after-effects may be eventually eliminated.' God! I wonder if mother has eliminated the worst after-effects!"

"She hasn't eliminated you anyway!" said Sally.

"Probably avoids it altogether. Marital relations. Wouldn't surprise me. Come and look at my new dress."

"You've another new dress? How many dresses can one girl have?"

"Quite a lot. I've got four now, four summer dresses, see!"

She flung open the door of her little wooden wardrobe and pulled out the dresses. Two were pink, one white with blue stripes, and one lemon.

"The blue and white pinstripe is the new one," she said, holding it up to her. "Do you like it?"

"It's beautiful," said Sally. "You're lucky. That's for Bundoran, is it?"

"Yes, for Bundoran. I'm really looking forward to it now, you know, I wasn't before. Manus wasn't going to come with us, he was going to stay and mind the shop, but now we've got someone else to take over while we're away, so he is coming. It's great. He really needs a break, he's been working so hard."

Sally did not know what she was supposed to say, so she said nothing.

"He's got some nice new things too. Would you like to see them?"

"Oh no," said Sally very quickly. "Not really. Has our visitor been over to see yours yet?" She changed the subject as quickly as she could

"No. Tell her to come some day, will you? Mother is dying to meet her. She seems so nice. I liked her hat, I must say, and she sounds interesting. Is she?"

"Yes, yes she is. She has all kinds of stories to tell. We're getting on very well with her. It's much better than I thought. Oh, that reminds me. My mother is getting married."

"Your mother? Who is she going to marry?"

"Packy Doherty."

Maura burst out laughing. She laughed until she was red in the face.

"I'm sorry," she spluttered. "I just can't help it. Packy Doherty. Oh my God! I can just see the two of them hobbling up the aisle. Oh goodness, it's too funny! I'll die laughing."

Sally smiled a bit to keep Maura company. For the second time she was speechless. It was one thing for her to criticise her mother's choice of mate, and another thing entirely to listen to Maura ridiculing it so heartily.

"You'll have a wedding to look forward to anyway," she said, when she stopped laughing. "When is the big day to be?"

"Oh, sometime in October."

"You'll have to get a new frock!" Maura started laughing again.

"Are you coming up the hill on Blaeberry Sunday?" Sally asked. Blaeberry Sunday was next Sunday, the last Sunday in July. Every year on this day the young people in Glenbra gathered at the foot of Knockageary, the highest mountain in the locality, and spent the day on its side, picking blueberries. When the berries were picked they had a picnic, and played and danced until late in the evening. Sally had not asked Manus if he were coming, but she assumed and hoped that he would. It would be an opportunity for them to be together in the company of other people of their own age. Until now they had always been alone together. Nothing could be better than to be alone with Manus, but Sally felt she would like to be with him in company as well. She would like people to see that she was Manus's girl. She would enjoy showing him off to all her old cronies from school. Manus was a boy any girl would be proud of.

But before the words were out of Maura's mouth Sally anticipated the answer.

"No," said Maura with what might have been a smug and knowing glance at Sally. "I'd love to, of course, but I'm not. We're going to spend the day at Eileen Carr's. She's invited all of us. There'll be a special Blaeberry Sunday lunch party there, with lots of people invited. They're going to have it out in the garden. The Carrs have such a beautiful garden, with a lily pond, you know, and little paths winding here and there through the grass. They've got a summer house even. I'd love a summer house. I'd love a garden, come to that, with a lily pond and a crazy paving path, oh, wouldn't it be heaven?"

13

Spin the Bottle

"So why do you have to go to Eileen Carr's? I thought you'd come with me up Knockageary just like everyone else. You always do that."

Sally and Manus were having a row.

Sally was upset and angry. She suspected she was being unreasonable but she did not know what to do about it. She suddenly felt that it was completely unfair of Manus not to spend Blaeberry Sunday with her and she could not understand why he would feel it was necessary to do just what his mother wanted.

"It's not my fault," he said calmly. Sally was crying and talking in a loud voice, but he remained completely calm. He was even smiling. He always smiled when he was under any sort of pressure, and never lost his temper like other, weaker, boys or men. Or girls or women. "We've got the invitation. My mother wants me to go. I can't back out of it without causing a huge fuss. It's only one afternoon, for heaven's sake."

"Yes. But it's an important afternoon. We never go anywhere together, it's always walking down to the beach, hiding from everyone. You think I'm a leper or something that has to be kept hidden."

"I don't. I love you."

"I love you too."

"Oh Manus. Manus, Manus, Manus!"

Sally loved to say Manus's name. She often said it to herself when she was alone, and she liked to address him by it when she was with him. But Manus seldom used her name. She could not recall him saying it more than once or twice. Sally. Her name. Why could he not say her name?

He kissed her, though.

"Don't get so upset about this. It's not worth it. We'll go somewhere when I come back from Bundoran. There'll be other things to go to."

"Like what?"

"I can't think now. But of course there will be lots of things."

"Your family hates me."

"I don't think they hate you. You're Maura's best friend, after all, more or less."

"Less if she thinks I've anything to do with you. They think I'm not good enough for you, don't they? It's not my fault that my father is dead and my mother is a poor widow who is just about to marry Packy Doherty. Or your fault that your father has struck lucky with that general store of his. God life is so unfair."

"Listen, don't think so much about all these things. What matters is you and me, isn't that it? Let's keep all this to ourselves for the moment, all right?"

"Oh Manus, what are we going to do? Can we run away together?"

"What do you mean, run away?"

"Elope. People do, if they love each other and aren't

allowed to get married."

He laughed and his eyes looked frightened.

"Go away out of that! I thought you were a sensible girl. Sensible girls don't elope. It's a sin. What we're doing now is a sin, even."

They were sitting arm in arm in a hollow rock.

"I don't care," said Sally. "It doesn't feel like a sin to me."

"And what about your mother, and Janey? You can't just run away from them. It's a cracked idea. I've got to stay and manage the store. Dad will give me a rise in wages at the end of the year. When I'm twenty-one he'll give me a share in the ownership of the shop. I can't just give all that up and elope!"

Much later, when she was grown up, Sally understood his point of view with regard to his job and his family and her responsibilities. She could see that her idea of running away from it all was crazy, when seen from that point of view. She knew later that he had loved her but could not make a great sacrifice on her behalf. He did not have enough faith in himself to take any wild unconventional step. Manus was the sort of person who relies only on his family and friends to tell him what is the right kind of behaviour, to tell him just what he should do in order to be a good and worthwhile human being. In this he was normal and not exceptional at all. He was all too normal and sensible when it came to the crunch, and all too unadventurous. There was nothing he could do, being what he was.

Later she understood all that. At the time she could only see that he did not love her as much as she loved him. And she thought he was being cowardly.

"I've found out what the message in the bottle was about, by the way," said Manus finding a happier subject of conversation.

"You did?" Sally rubbed the tears out of her eyes. "What is it about, then?"

"It's amazing. It's not a prisoner, or someone on a desert island, or anything exciting like that. Can you believe it was thrown into the sea off the coast of America, by someone working in the American Institute of Marine Meteorology division to trace the flow of the Gulf Stream. Have you heard of the Gulf Stream?"

"No. I don't think so."

"Well, it's a stream, a current, of warm water. It flows out of the Gulf of Mexico, in America, across the Atlantic, and along the coast of Europe. It makes the sea around Ireland warmer than it would be otherwise. And it makes the climate warmer here too. Isn't it interesting?"

"Yes, it is."

"And in order to see where it flows they threw these bottles in it hoping that they'd be carried across the sea in the stream and land on the shores of the places it goes to, if you see what I mean. I have to write to this person, the one whose name is in the bottle, and tell him I found it, and where."

"Will you tell him I found it too?"

Manus grinned. He thought that was a joke, and seemed to have forgotten that Sally was the one who had tripped over the bottle originally.

She didn't press the point.

"Who told you all this?"

"Well, I showed it to my father, and he showed it to one of the police constables in town, and he knew, somehow. They're doing a piece about it in the newspaper.

They already have. Look I'll show it to you, I have it here in my pocket."

He pulled out a page of newspaper and showed Sally the article:

Glenbra Youth Finds American Bottle On Beach

On 29 June Manus McLoughlin of Glenbra stumbled on a wine bottle on the beach at Glenbra Brae.The bottle was thrown into the sea off the coast of Mexico in July 1891 by an officer with the American Hydrographic Office carrying out research on the Gulf Stream.

Master McLoughlin said "I did not know what it was at first. It was a great surprise. I am writing to the Hydrographic Office to tell them where I found it."

"That's great," said Sally. "Getting your name in the paper and all. You must be pleased about that."

"Oh it's not so important," he shrugged. "I'd like to know more about the Gulf Stream, though. I've asked them to send me some information. I'd like to know more about the sea in general."

Bridgie Greene was just managing to survive in the yellow hut. July was a hard month for everyone: the new harvest was not in, and for many people the food from last year was already used up. Bridgie, needless to remark, was one of those who had run out of supplies early in June.

"And now I don't have any crops to harvest!" she said to Sally. "My field of oats and my garden of taties are both gone."

They were eating soup made of grain which some neighbours, including Mrs Gallagher, who had little enough to spare, had given them, that mixed with wild mustard, or *praiseach* as it was called.

"It's supposed to be nourishing," said Bridgie. "But it tastes awful and the children are getting yellow skin. Just look at wee Dónal!"

Dónal was looking less well than he had at the time of the eviction. He had grown thin, and his skin did look terrible. It was a jaundiced yellow colour.

"The bigger ones will be home come November," said Sally comfortingly. "They'll have some money for you from the potato harvest across the water, and then you'll be set up for the winter. Will they go into service again? I suppose they will have to."

Bridgie's eldest children, even though the youngest of them was only nine, had gone to Scotland for the harvest, picking potatoes. This meant she had fewer mouths to feed and could look forward to the money they would bring back with them at the end of their spell in Scotland.

"Och, of course they'll have to. They are our only hope. Just like you and Katie were for your mother, God bless you. She's doing so well now, but she has less to worry about than me. She's a lucky woman, only had the three of you."

"Do you ever hear from them in Scotland?" asked Sally, dandling Dónal on her knee. He was a lovely little boy, smiling and laughing all the time.

"I'd a letter from Mary the first week they went but nothing since then. She said they'd arrived safely and the place was all right. That's all. Sure the poor things are probably too tired to write, God love them. It's terrible having to send off little Annie like that, and her only nine years of age."

"She's young, all right, for Scotland."

"You're the lucky girl, never had to do that. And you struck well for yourself in Tyrone."

"I was lucky there. But lots of people are lucky with their places. Your children are too, just wait and see. I brought you over some yellow meal, look. Here, you can have some real porridge tonight. And we're pulling the potatoes on Saturday. I'll bring over a bag then, Mother says she wants to."

"We'll have our Blaeberry dinner then anyway. You are very good to me. I suppose you'll be off up Knockageary on Sunday?" She laughed. The Blaeberry Sunday outing was one of the best times of the year for boys and girls to get together. It was well known that it was a time for flirting and finding a boy or a girl for yourself.

"I suppose so." Sally was not happy to be reminded of the nature of the occasion.

"Sure maybe you have a young man for yourself already, never mind the blaeberries at all!"

Sally laughed weakly. She felt guilty whenever any hint of her friendship with Manus was given by anyone. She didn't know who knew about it but guessed that some people must. In one way she wanted the whole world to know and in another the thought of it being common knowledge scared her. It was as if she were ashamed of it and did not deserve to have Manus's attention. It was as if she, as much as his family, by now believed what they held, namely that she was not good enough for him.

She began to sing a song to Dónal to take her mind off the question:

"Trup trup my little horse,
Trup trup my darling!
Trup trup my little horse
Prancing down the roadway!"

While she sang she bounced him up and down on her knee, up and down, faster and faster, until he laughed his head off and screamed for mercy.

14

Blaeberry Sunday

*T*he corn in the field in front of the house was yellow gold. Cornflowers fluttered on its surface like blue butterflies. Under the stone walls at the edges of the field other flowers nodded: white ox-eye daisies, red poppies, yellow buttercups. The crop of oats in the next field was darker: burnished, the colour of bronze. Rich green leaves spread like umbrellas across the potato patch behind the house, and in the garden the gooseberries and blackcurrants were fat and ripe, ready for picking.

It was an early harvest, and, in spite of the scarcity of rain, promised to be a good one.

On the day before Blaeberry Sunday Mrs Gallagher and Sally, with Janey and the Visitor as onlookers, went out to the potato patch and ceremonially picked a basinful of new potatoes. They knew the potatoes were sound: Mrs Gallagher had been keeping a wary eye on them all summer. Still, there was a moment of suspense when she dug out the first root and shook the dry clay off the five or six potatoes that clung to it. They were small tubers, not yet fully grown, and were irregular and shapeless. The kind of potato called, appropriately, "Lumpers". When sliced in two with a knife in the kitchen, they showed clean white flesh.

"Not a mark!" said Mrs Gallagher. "They're perfect, thanks be to God and his Holy Mother for that."

"Hooray!" cried the Visitor. "Hooray, hooray! Let's hope everyone's are the same."

"And that they stay like that," said Mrs Gallagher. She could remember that last year the first few potatoes were good, but that as the season had progressed the blight destroyed most of them. This year, however, there was no hint that anything was amiss.

She put pessimistic thoughts from her mind as she boiled the potatoes and prepared bacon, cabbage, and a gooseberry dumpling, for a special dinner which would celebrate the harvest and also mark the end of the Visitor's stay in Glenbra. Miss Bannister was going back to Dublin the next day.

"The time has gone so fast!" said the Visitor. "I can't believe that I am going home tomorrow. Have I really been here for four weeks, or was it all a heavenly dream?"

"It's good that you've enjoyed it," said Sally. "Your Irish has improved a lot, too."

Not that that would have been hard, she added privately. Sally had spent an hour a day teaching the Visitor the rudiments of the language. By now she could carry on a very simple conversation about a simple domestic subject, such as what she was going to eat for dinner, or the weather. And her accent was good: she had an ear for language.

"Thanks to you, Sally. Well, once I go back to Dublin I'll start to take classes. The Gaelic League is organising a whole series of them for the winter, I will be very very busy. It's something to look forward to. Otherwise I will die of loneliness."

"Oh dear," said Sally and Mrs Gallagher simultaneously, as the Visitor allowed a tear to roll down her cheek – by now much browner and healthier-looking than it had been when she first came.

"It's just that I'm going to miss you all so much. I've loved it here. I've never been happier, to tell you the truth."

"A year will go round soon enough," consoled Mrs Gallagher. "Would you like another of these potatoes now, and a wee dollop of butter?"

"Thank you, thank you. The potatoes are delicious. I've never tasted any so delicious, the whole meal is just perfect, a feast fit for a king. It truly is."

"It is our feast, our feast for the first harvest," said Sally. "It should be good."

"You don't know how lucky you are," said the Visitor, "to live here in this heavenly place, among lovely people. Speaking your own language and eating this fresh, good food."

"Well, yes, it is nice sometimes," said Sally.

"I know. You are thinking of Katie, on hire. And those girls of the Greenes, in Scotland, tatie hoking. The poverty is a problem, I can understand that. But in spite of it you have so much that is good. I can understand that you would never want to leave it."

"Sally may have to leave it," said Mrs Gallagher, with a sigh. "Most young people here do leave."

"You should stay, Sally, if you can."

"I would like to," said Sally, also sighing.

"And if you don't you should come to Dublin. Don't go to Scotland, or America, or Canada. Come to Dublin. If you ever need a job write to me and I'll get you one. My goodness, you could do so well in Dublin now. Why didn't I think of it before? You could get a job as a nurse or a governess to some family who want their children to learn Irish. You could talk to people at the classes . . . You really ought to come."

"Well . . . "

A few seconds ago she was saying that she really ought to stay!

"Do write and let me know. You must promise me that. Do not go to any of those other awful places, stay in your own country. At least do that much. Promise?"

"Of course I will promise that," said Sally. "It sounds like something I would like to do, if I do not stay here. I will certainly write if I need a job."

Blaeberry Sunday. After Mass all the boys and girls were shouting invitations to one another: "Are you going to the hill?" "See you on the hill!" They were nudging and winking and biffing one another, anticipating the pleasures ahead. Sally did not want to go. She had missed Blaeberry Sunday last year, and this morning her thoughts were poisoned by jealousy. As soon as she had woken up she had thought of Manus heading off to Eileen Carr's house. She could see him and Maura, dressed up to the nines, standing on the close cut grass of the Carr's lawn, drinking lemonade. What would Eileen be wearing? Something beautiful – hadn't Maura talked about a silk dress, or some flowing muslin thing, flimsy and seductive? She could see them talking together, then strolling off under the trees, laughing, enjoying one another's company. Manus's parents looking on, nodding their approval. Eileen Carr. Such a sweet charming girl! So respectable, so nice! So rich! Just what they wanted for Manus.

She could see them going in the evening to the Blaeberry outing at Ranny Hill, near where Eileen lived. There would be melodeons playing, fiddles. She could see Eileen and Manus dancing as she wanted to dance with him . . .

Stop! she had to shout to herself, inside her mind. Stop! None of this will happen. It'll probably be a dull afternoon with all the parents and old people there spoiling the fun.

The worst of it was she would not see Manus now, or even Maura, for more than a week. For nearly two weeks. She would not find out until then what had happened and whether it had all been as delightful as Maura had foreseen, or whether it had been disappointing. Or anything.

"I'll be there!" Sally shouted automatically at a boy, Michael something or other, who yelled at her about the Knockageary outing. "I'll be there," she said to herself. "Go, for heaven's sake. If you stay at home thinking about things you will go mad."

At two o'clock or thereabouts the boys and girls, and some older people, such as Mrs Gallagher, who had brought Janey along, assembled at the foot of the hill. They were dressed in their Sunday clothes, and carrying lunchbags, pandies or noggins, buckets and skillets, for collecting berries in. Some had brought no utensil but planned to spike the berries with a long stalk or a rush and carry them in that way, all strung together like beads on a necklace. A few of the boys carried musical instruments.

Sally met Elizabeth Gallagher, back from her aunt's, and a few girls she had gone to school with, some of whom she had not seen much of recently. She was shy meeting them at first, but soon began to enjoy listening to their conversation.

They all began to climb the hill. Knockageary, the highest mountain in Glenbra, was still not all that high. It was less than three thousand feet. It sloped very gradually at first, and there were some tracks made by turf-cutters which made it easy to make the first half of the ascent. At about a half way point the mountain grew considerably steeper until it finally rounded off, rather than peaked. Right on top of the mountain was a stone megalith, a dolmen.

The lower slopes of the mountain were thickly covered with heather, interspersed by patches of gorse and occasional emerald green stretches of marshy land. The heather was dry as paper, and so thick that it covered every other plant that mingled with it, including the low-lying blueberry bushes.

The boys and girls walked with eyes bent to the heather, looking out for the fine reddish leaves and the little blue-black berries which taste more delicious than any other wild berry. They knew that the best place for blueberries was about half way up the hill, but they kept their eyes skinned just the same for fear of missing any on the lower slopes. Whenever Sally found a berry she popped it into her mouth, forgetting about the pandy which she had promised to fill for Granny. Mrs Gallagher and Janey were trailing along behind her, with Janey prancing around in the sunshine, loving every minute of the fun.

They stopped at a flattish ledge half way up the hill where the blueberries grew in great abundance. Sally picked rapidly, filling her can. Mrs Gallagher stretched out on the heather, idly eating the berries that grew around her. Janey was playing chasing with some other children, and a group of boys were trying to play pitch and toss on a flat piece of rocky ground. The older girls started singing as they picked, the song they always sang first on Blaeberry Sunday: *"Thugamar féin an sambradh linn!"*

"Summertime, summertime,
Milk of the kine!
We have brought the summer with us!
Summertime, summertime,
Laughter and wine
We have brought the summer with us!"

The song filtered over the hillside like fairy music. Sally watched her mother in her white Sunday blouse, her skirt half hidden in the spiky purple heather, her face calm and happy as she looked at Janey playing. And at all the boys and girls like flowers dotted over the hillside. Sunshine, laughter, song. It was like a vision of paradise.

When the pandies were full, the mountain's crop of blueberries depleted, the lunchbags were taken out and everyone ate whatever they had: bread and butter, mostly. Lucky people had barm brack. They washed it down with milk or cold tea. It all tasted much better out here on the mountain than it would inside in a hot kitchen.

After the picnic, the group split up. The teenagers were going to continue to climb the mountain, and when they reached the top they would have their own party there. The younger children and the older people would stay just where they were or else begin the descent homeward: most of them did not want to complete the last and hardest part of the ascent. And they would not be welcome to do so. There was an unwritten rule that the party on top of the hill was for the young fry exclusively. Indeed, it was one of the few occasions during the year when they had a party of their own completely free of adult supervision. They had been looking forward to it for weeks.

Sally hesitated. But her mother persuaded her to continue up the mountain with Elizabeth and the others.

"Go on out of that!" she said. "You need a bit of fun. It'll be good for you."

Sally thought guiltily that her mother did not have the faintest idea that she was "carrying on" with Manus. She wished she did, and resolved to tell her about it all as soon as Manus came back from his holiday.

Manus. What a pity he wasn't here! She began to feel sorry for him. Nothing could be as pleasant as this. He was the one to be pitied, not her.

She would enjoy telling him all about it.

"Here, Sally, can I give you a hand there!" It was that Michael fellow, offering to help her across a stretch covered with prickly gorse, which smelled like burnt honey but scratched viciously.

"Ah go away with you, Michael," she knew what the expected banter was. "I can manage that well enough on my own and well you know it!"

The rest of the day was going to be one long exercise in flirtation. You could already see the crowd splintering into couples, some – girls and boys who had already been going together – closing in immediately the grown-ups were left behind, others more tentative, hovering in the vicinity of one another, testing the ground. And then there were the boys and girls who were not attached to anyone, whose hearts were free and who were here for the crack and the fun of not knowing what might happen.

Michael was one of those. Or maybe he had had his

eye on Sally from earlier on?

She hoped not.

"Ah, Sally, don't be cruel!" he called good-humouredly.

"All right then Michael. Come along and help me. You can carry me across if you like, but I'm telling you I'm a hefty lump, ten stones weight and more. I don't think you're able for me at all!"

"I'm well able for you, Sally my girl, you just wait now and see!" He bounded across to where she was, swept her up in his arms and began to stride across the patch of gorse. He was barefoot, like most of them, but the skin on his feet and legs was so tough that the gorse hardly bothered him.

"Ach, Michael, I was only joking so I was. Put me down this minute or I'll let out a roar that'll frighten the life out of everyone!"

"I'll put you down when you're at the other side, and not one minute sooner," he said, rather firmly.

Sally had to put up with that, and she didn't mind it at all. Nobody, naturally enough, had carried her in this way since she was about two years old. She couldn't possibly remember that far back. But it seemed to her that she did, and that she could recall Jack, her father, carrying her across the fields in his arms, just as Michael was now. It felt precarious, comforting and wildly funny, all at the same time.

In this spirit the ascent continued. The crowd of girls and boys stumbled, sang, and joked, but mainly flirted, their way to the top of the mountain.

There was a mad race at the end to see who would reach to top first and climb up on the dolmen. Finally about five or six boys seemed to reach this zenith together, and risking life and limb, they stood together on the flat stone across the top, shouting at the tops of their voices.

The dolmen had been on Knockageary for thousands of years. So everyone said. People called it "*Leaba Diarmada agus Ghráinne*", the bed of Diarmaid and Gráinne. The story was that it was one of the beds Diarmaid and Gráinne, two lovers eloping, had slept on during their flight from Fionn, the leader of the Fianna, a band of hunters. He was an old man but he wanted to marry Gráinne himself. He chased them across Ireland, and they stopped to rest at many places, always sleeping in the open air, apparently, if the stories were to be believed, on slabs of rock which looked decidedly uncomfortable. In the end Fionn had got them. Diarmaid was killed by a boar, the only animal that had the power to kill him.

Three of the boys who were musicians sat under the dolmen and began to play their instruments: melodeon, fiddle and tin whistle. They played jigs and reels, and the girls and boys danced together, enjoying the fresh air up here on top of the world, enjoying the difficulty of dancing on the uneven ground, enjoying their freedom to be together.

That is to say, most of them appeared to be enjoying that freedom. Michael asked Sally to dance as soon as the music started. Then he asked her again, and again. He was a nice boy. That's what Sally thought. A nice boy, with nice black hair and a nice brown face. And a polite boy and a kind boy.

But he was not Manus. He wouldn't do.

When he asked her up for the fourth dance she said: "Why don't you give Elizabeth a turn? She's been sitting here twiddling her thumbs for the past half hour."

Michael looked aggrieved, but did as he was told. He and Elizabeth, who was a good-looking girl but too quiet to attract much attention from the boys, joined the crowd. They danced together in solemn silence. Sally observed them for a while: maybe, eventually, she would manage to start talking. Maybe, eventually, he would notice how pretty she was, and what a lovely girl. Oh well, they would have to look out for themselves in this game. Sally certainly had enough to do looking out for herself. After a while she turned her back on the dancing, and, sitting on a tussock at a remove from the crowd, she gazed down at the view of the valley far below them now, and at the sea behind it.

The dance music stopped, and one of the girls – it was Sadie McFadden, who had a cast in her eye and long perfectly yellow hair – sang. She sang the saddest song there is, "Dónal Óg".

"You promised me, and you told a lie to me,
    That you would meet me behind the shieling
    I whistled once, and called out loud to you
    But all I heard was the lambs' high bleating."

Sadie had a magical voice. It was strong and powerful, but carried the poignant notes of the song delicately, giving full vent to their tragic tone. Sally started to cry. This song always made her feel sad. Now, as Sadie sang about the girl who had given her heart completely to a boy who then left her, she felt all her anxiety about Manus and all her love for him well up inside her. Manus loved her. He had not left her. But she felt she was that girl in the song. She understood exactly how she felt, how sad it was that her love had not felt the same way.

"You promised you would give me what is impossible
    That you would give me shoes of birdskin

That you would give me gloves of fishskin
And a suit of the finest silk in Ireland."

He had felt the same way at first, and then changed his mind. Could people change their minds about something like that? About something as important as love? Sally let the tears flow. She couldn't stop them.

The song was quite long. It went on for ten verses. Sally cried until stanza eight and then, feeling a bit better, she rubbed her eyes with her hand. She would have time to hide the traces of tears by the time the song was finished.

She glanced down the hillside and then rubbed her eyes again.

An angel was flying up the mountain. That's what it looked like, anyway. A white figure, gleaming in the dusk, was coming up the mountain at a speed which was not possible for an ordinary human being.

Closer and closer it came, at alarming speed. It seemed to be rolling now, tumbling, spinning.

"Oh God!" said Sally, starting to laugh. "Oh my God! I know who it is!"

He cartwheeled for the final leg of the ascent. Have you ever seen someone cartwheeling up a mountainside? It is an impressive sight.

"Hello Sally!" he said. "It's Blaeberry Sunday. Here I am!"

"Hello Olaf," she said. "Welcome to Knockageary."

15

Olaf of the Many Crafts

Olaf had come to help with the harvest.

"I said I would come, did I not?" he looked perplexed, when Sally expressed surprise at his arrival.

"I forgot," said Sally. "But it's good of you to come. It is nice to see you again."

As soon as Olaf arrived she had felt her spirit lighten just as it had the first time she met him. It was miraculous. He was such a clown that nobody could be heavy-hearted when he was around.

"Where are you going to stay?" she asked. She could hardly picture him in her own house. He looked stranger than ever. He was still wearing his wide white trousers and white shirt with the addition of a wide black belt around his waist. He had a large black hat, with lots of things stuck under the ribbon: a penknife, pencils, a ruler, even a mouth organ, which he pulled down from time to time and played very tunefully. On his back was a red and blue spotted bundle which he had not opened yet.

"What do you have in it?" Sally asked. There was no need to be coy with Olaf. Indeed it would have been unthinkable. She knew after two minutes acquaintance that in spite of his eccentricity he was the most completely straightforward person she had ever met.

"My worldly goods," he said. "Do you want to see them now?"

"No no," said Sally. "That's all right. I suppose it's just your clothes and things?"

"I am wearing my clothes," he said. "It is things. Look, I will show you."

He pulled down the bundle and opened it. Hundreds of objects tumbled out. There was a fishing line, hooks and some brightly coloured flies. A school notebook. A square piece of white fur. A lump of red rock. A hammer. A bag of nails. A smelly piece of dried fish. A rabbit snare. A compass. A lump of brown sugar candy. And many other things.

"See!" he said, pulling out the candy. "Do you know what this is?"

"It's rock," said Sally. "Of course I know what it is. Brown rock."

"It's yellow man," said Olaf. "That is what it is."

And he put his hand on his hip and sang:

"At the ould Lammas Fair
Were you ever ever there
Were you ever at the fair in Ballycastle Oh?
Did you treat your Mary Ann
To bread and Yellow Man
At the ould Lammas Fair in Ballycastle Oh?"

"Here, have some, Sally Anne!" he said, with a sweeping bow, placing the lump of sticky stuff on her lap.

"How do you know my name is Sally Anne?"

"I know. It is, is it not?"

"It is indeed. Were you at the ould Lammas Fair then?"

"I was not. It is on tomorrow I believe. But I was in ould Ballycastle Oh three days ago and the yellow man was already available. I got it for you, Sally Anne! Do you know what this is?"

He pulled out the square of fur.

Sally caressed it. It was very soft, and snowy white.

"Polar bear skin," he said, triumphantly.

"Ah yes, there are polar bears in Iceland, of course."

"No, not in Iceland, but in Greenland. I have been to Greenland fishing and I got a polar bear skin there."

"Did you kill the bear yourself?"

"No. I got it from a Greenlander. An Eskimo. The people you thought lived in Iceland."

"So. It's Greenland they live in?"

"It is."

Olaf told her about the Eskimos who live in Greenland and live all their lives in the snow, hunting seals and walruses and bears and living only on fish and meat. He told her about Iceland, its glaciers and volcanoes, and springs of water which were boiling hot, bubbling like hot baths in the ground. He told her that the nicest thing an Icelandic boy can do for a girl is prepare a bath for her out in the middle of the bog, so that she can sit and soak in the hot water under the summer sky.

"Go away out of that!" said Sally. "You're just codding me so you are."

Olaf laughed.

"It is so. I will tell you more tomorrow. Now I must sleep."

"Ah yes," said Sally.

"I thought I would sleep at your house. Since I have

124

come to help you with the harvest that seems only right."

"Yes, well . . . I suppose it does."

Sally let him come along with her. She did not know how she was going to explain him to her mother but she did not have to worry about that. Olaf did all the explaining himself.

"I am Olaf Baldursson," he said. "I have come from Iceland to Killybegs on a fishing boat, and now I am going to help you with the harvest."

"But . . . "

"You need help?"

"We could do with a hand."

"I am a friend of your daughter, Sally. We met at the hiring fair in Rathmullan in May and I told her I would come and help. So here I am. Can I sleep here tonight? I have nowhere else to go."

"You look so . . . Are you a gypsy?"

"I am not a gypsy. I am a fisherman. And many other things. I would like to help you and I can do lots of things. I can fix your thatch, for instance. It needs fixing. And I can mend that crane over the fire. It is dangerous, broken like that. But of course, if you are suspicious and worried about me, I will be happy to go away. I do not want to upset you at all."

"Oh no no no, you're not upsetting me, of course you are not upsetting me. I've never met an Icelander before, I don't think I have. Although maybe I did once, I think now there was a boat from there, somewhere like that, once in Rathmullan. Yes. Would you have some tea now like a good boy?"

"Thank you. That would be very nice."

Olaf stayed, sleeping on the floor of the parlour. He could have had the Visitor's bed but Sally had already been restored to that and anyway he said he preferred to sleep on a floor. It was what he was used to.

The next day the Gallaghers started to cut their corn. A small *meitheal* came to help them, but since everyone in Glenbra who had any crops was anxious to harvest them before they overripened, it was a very small one. Packy Doherty was there, and Madge's man, Miley. Otherwise just Sally, Janey, Mrs Gallagher and Olaf.

First, Packy – and this symbolised his new status with the Gallaghers – picked one ear of corn and pulled a few grains from it. He bit into them, tasted them, and then spit them out on the ground.

"It's ready," he said. "Good and ready."

A long speech, for Packy.

At his word, Olaf and Miley took up their sickles and began to reap. Sally and Mrs Gallagher and Janey walked behind them. As the corn was cut, they gathered it into sheaves and bound each sheaf with a stalk. They would be left then to dry out in the sun.

"It's a pity the Visitor is gone. She would have enjoyed doing this and no mistake," said Mrs Gallagher, wiping sweat from her forehead.

"Next year she should stay for the two months, shouldn't she?" said Sally. "But you and Packy will be married then, of course. You won't be living here any more."

"Och, we haven't made up our minds which house we'll live in, we haven't decided that at all yet. I'm not sure, his is bigger but I think ours is nicer myself and I think maybe Granny would like to stay in it. Old folk never like to be shunted about."

"That's true."

But would Packy like to be shunted about? Sally looked

at him. He wasn't old in the same sense as Granny was, of course, he was probably only about fifty or so. Today he was looking his best, dressed in an old blue shirt with the sleeves rolled up, old tweed trousers tied at the waist with a bit of string. He swung the sickle with wide, rhythmical sweeps. This was something he did even better than Olaf, who was so good at everything according to himself. He was managing very well, too, although he had no experience of reaping. There was no corn in Iceland. The climate was too cold for it. But he had cut hay. The knack of using the sickle was different from that of wielding the bigger, cruder scythe, but perhaps not all that different. As long as you had strong forearms you could manage either.

The three men worked well together. They stood about two or three yards apart, Olaf, all in white, in the middle, and the two older men on either side of him. Each reaped away himself but they kept an even pace. Behind them the paths of shorn corn lay, fragrant and fresh, waiting to be picked up and bound by the women.

Sally and her mother continued to chat as they worked together. They had not had such a good talk in a long time: the work, the open air, the smell of the cut corn, helped Sally to be warmer and more open with Mrs Gallagher than she usually was. Even though they talked they worked hard, stooping and binding, stooping and binding. Janey had given up after about half an hour: she had found a frog whose leg had been broken by the sickle and was busy nursing it.

"Poor wee frog!" she said, cradling the brownish creature in her hands. It looked up at her with shiny bulging eyes. "Janey make you better!" She carried her patient to the edge of the field and made a bed for it under the wall. As soon as she put the frog to bed, it hopped rapidly away, broken leg and all.

Janey was not upset.

"The frog got better!" she said. "I made him better."

Then she wandered about in search of a replacement. As there were dozens of frogs in the field she found more than one, although not all of them had broken legs and most of them were able to hop away before her little pink hands grabbed them and carried them away.

At noon, when it was really too hot to keep going, Sally went back to the house and fetched a can of tea and milk and a big plate of soda bread and butter. Her back was aching and she felt exhausted. She washed her hot face in the rain water barrel and fastened her handkerchief under her hair, and that refreshed her a little. The picnic lunch, eaten at the side of the field sitting on the new stubble, refreshed her even more. All the reapers were in a good mood. They had worked well, more than a third of the field was already cut. They drank their milk and ate their bread, laughing and chatting, promising each other that they would have this field done by lunchtime tomorrow and the oatfield by Thursday.

"By the end of next week we'll have the flax cut!" said Packy Doherty. "If the weather holds."

They all looked up at the sun blazing in the clear sky.

"The weather will hold!" they said. "With the help of God!"

16

Tragedy

Sally was so tired at the end of the first day in the field that she could do nothing, think of nothing, talk about nothing. All she could do was go to bed and sleep one of the soundest sleeps of her life. Her dreams were all about cornfields. Cornfields as wide and long as the sea, stretching without fences or ditches for miles and miles. She and Manus were walking through them. But she was reaping, Manus was walking along not doing anything. In the end he simply vanished and she was continuing to move through the field, swinging her reaping hook, cutting her way through the endless corn.

On the second evening she felt less tired. Her body had grown more accustomed to the exercise and no longer felt as if it was made of jelly. She went to see Bridgie Greene to bring her a bag of spuds as she had promised. Olaf went along with her.

Bridgie had made the little hut spick and span. The two little girls were playing outside, and were delighted when Olaf presented them with two dollies which he had twisted from some corn stalks. When he stayed outside and did a few handstands for them, they were even more delighted.

Bridgie was very pleased with the potatoes.

"A thousand thanks to you," she said. "Everyone is being very good to me, I'm doing fine, but it's great to have a whole bag of new spuds. That'll keep us going for weeks."

Bridgie was looking well. Her skin was clear and her eyes sparkled. Even her clothes seemed less ragged than usual: she had a white blouse with her black skirt, which suited her dark complexion very well. She'd had a letter from her daughter in Scotland: "They are doing fine, she says. They've plenty to eat and the work is hard but they're all right, they're having a good time. The McAllisters treat them well."

But she was worried about her youngest.

"Dónal is sick," she said. "I don't know what's wrong with the poor wee thing. He's not in bed, mind you, and he has no fever. But he's not thriving any more."

Sally felt her heart sink. Bridgie did not need more troubles.

"Where is he?" she asked.

Bridgie called and Dónal, who had been playing out at the back of the hut, came in. Sally closed her eyes for a second when she saw him. She was shocked. He was as yellow as a dandelion, and he had lost a lot of weight.

"Hello, how is my wee pet?" she said. He smiled and came over to her. She took him on her lap.

"How is my good, good little pet? The best wee boy in Ireland? The best wee boy in Europe? The best wee boy in the whole world?"

Dónal laughed and Sally pulled his ear. He was skin and bone, he hardly weighed anything.

"Did you meet my funny foreign friend?" she asked.

Dónal hadn't.

"Wait a minute now, I'll bring you out to him."

Sally carried Dónal to the door of the hut and called to Olaf, who was standing on his head, much to the amusement of the girls and the consternation of the dog.

"Olaf, I've someone for you to meet," she called.

Olaf righted himself and Sally introduced him very formally to Dónal.

"Now, you'll teach Dónal some useful tricks, won't you, while I talk to Bridgie?"

Olaf took one look at Dónal, who was standing holding Sally's hand, and nodded. He picked the little boy up and started to talk to him.

"Do you know how to tell a rabbit's footprints? No? I will tell you . . . "

Sally went back into the hut.

"Has he been eating?"

"Well, for a while we had nothing but the *praiseach* and the bit of meal, and none of them would eat much of that. Now we've got flour and bread but he has little appetite for it. He only ate a couple of blaeberries on Sunday."

"Maybe the potatoes will do him good. Have you any drop of milk at all?"

Bridgie looked ashamed.

"Only the odd drop that somebody gives us. Milk might do him a power of good . . . "

"I'll bring you some. I'll bring you milk every day."

"Och, Sally. You can't spare it, you've got plenty for your own milk."

"We can spare it if he's sick. Of course we can. Sure anyone would give you a drop of milk for the poor sick child if you'd only ask. You're too proud."

131

"What else is there to be?"

"Well, I know what you mean. But I'll bring over the milk now every day, and maybe in a short while Dónal will be fat and healthy again."

"With the help of God," said Bridgie. "I couldn't stand to lose him. You know he's always so bold and so funny, but he's always been the best wean . . . he was the loveliest baby. Smiling when he was a few weeks old and quicker walking and talking than any of them. He was three months when Turlough was killed. That's all, he never knew his Daddy at all. But he was such a lovely child he helped me get over it. That's the truth."

"I know. Mother feels like that about Janey."

"I suppose it's always the baby that you feel like that about. It's not that I don't love the others. I love them all just as much. But . . . "

"He'll be all right," said Sally. "He will be better. Just wait and see."

Sally came every morning, as soon as she'd milked Rose, with a pandy of milk. She brought butter sometimes too, if they'd churned, and a bit of oaten bread fresh from the griddle. Anything she thought might tempt Dónal's appetite.

Olaf came with Sally or else visited the hut alone in the evenings. He knew something about healing and he made a medicine from herbs which he gathered in the ditches.

"It will strengthen his blood," he said. "I think there is something the matter with the boy's blood."

The medicine did not taste very nice and Dónal hated it. But he took it nevertheless.

"It will make you feel better."

"Not sick Mammy, I'm not sick."

"You'll feel stronger. You'll be able to eat the nice cake Sally brings, and you'll be able to go swimming again on the shore."

That persuaded him.

"Do you think he's mending?" Sally asked Bridgie, after a week or so of this treatment.

"Aye, I think he's getting a bit better," said Bridgie. "Today he came for a wee walk with me over the road, you know. He hasn't been able to do that for a while."

"You don't think you should get the doctor?"

"The doctor is it? Och no, I don't think there's any need for that."

Bridgie would not have called the doctor unless she thought Dónal was going to die. She had never called the doctor for any of her children.

Sally thought Dónal looked not worse, but not much better. She played with him and tried to feed him, but always left the Greene's hut with a heavy heart.

The McLoughlins were due back from Bundoran.

Sally was so busy with the harvesting that she had little time for visiting. In the evenings she sometimes looked under the oak tree, thinking Manus might be there. But he never was. She felt uneasy, but was so occupied with everything that was going on that she did not get really worried. Eventually Maura came to call on her. So they were back.

"We'd a marvellous holiday," she said. "It was so much fun. My aunt's guest house, *Railway View*, was really excellent. I had my own room and we had rashers and eggs for breakfast every morning, and white and black pudding, and the promenade was just beautiful."

"When did you get back?"

"Oh, we got back a few days ago. On Saturday, we came back. We travelled with the Carrs. They were there too, on holidays in Bundoran. They were staying at another guest house, a hotel really. But we spent a lot of time with them, we went to supper with them once and dancing and everything."

"How was the party at Carrs'?"

"The party?"

"On Blaeberry Sunday."

"Oh, that! So much has happened since then I'd forgotten all about it. It was fine. It was a good party. Yes. Afterwards we went to the dancing at Ranny Hill, and that was good too. I danced with John Carr, actually."

"How is Manus?"

For once, Sally could not resist asking about him. Her heart felt as if it was made of sponge and was being squeezed by a tight fist.

Maura looked anxious and a bit shy.

"Manus? Oh he's very well," she said. "He had a good time too. He's walking out with Eileen Carr now. I suppose you guessed that? It's been going on, really, for a long time, you know, all the time you were away in Tyrone. But now it seems to be official if you know what I mean."

For once Maura sounded sympathetic. That made it all worse. Sally knew she had been anticipating this moment for weeks. She had tried to tell herself that she was being unreasonable and pessimistic, but her dreams and her intuitions had been right, and her logical mind had been wrong. The worst thing, the thing she feared more than anything else, the thing she thought was so terrible that it could not possibly happen to her, had happened. And it felt just as bad as Sally had anticipated. Nothing in her life had ever felt as painful, not the death of her father, not leaving home to go to the hiring fair. Nothing. And nothing in her life afterwards would ever feel so bad either. But she did not know that then, as she sat in her kitchen with Maura and tried to pretend she was totally unconcerned about Manus one way or the other, or afterwards, as she ran across the stubble field to the old sycamore tree where she used to read, and buried her face in the soft grass that grew under its shade.

17

More of the Same

*S*ally had to talk to someone about it. So she talked to Olaf. "I can't understand why he would do it," she sobbed. She could not talk about it without crying. "We were so happy together."

"Yes," for once he looked at a loss. "It is very sad. But these things happen all the time. It happens to everyone."

"It . . . does . . . not . . . happen . . . to . . . everyone!" said Sally, who refused to be comforted by clichés. Olaf was not the one to use clichés, that was why she turned to him.

"Perhaps not everyone. But it happens to a lot of people."

"Why?"

"I do not know."

"We were so happy!"

"Were you?"

"Yes. Of course I was worried and all that. But in between I had the happiest moments of my whole life. And he did too. I know he did."

"He is a practical person."

"He will do what his mamma and papa expect, oh yes, and they do not expect him to hitch himself up with a no-good servant girl like me."

"You see, he is not perfect."

"I know he is not perfect. I never said he was perfect. But I loved him anyway. I do love him anyway. I understand him. I could have helped him. I could have been good for him."

"But could he have been good for you?"

"He was very good for me. If he'd let himself be."

"But he couldn't let himself?"

"No. There was something in him. Some knot, some barrier. I don't know. He was pulling against me."

"There you are. He was not good for you. You do not need someone to pull against you. Life is good at doing that anyway."

"Ah . . . " Sally got tired talking about it. She just wanted to cry. After a while she got tired of crying too, and then she just lay with her head on her pillow. Empty.

The next day she said: "I'll go and see him. I'll talk to him about it."

Last night, when she had felt too sad even to cry she had promised herself this, that she would go and talk to him. Surely that was not too much to ask? Girls were not supposed to be pushy, they were not supposed to ask questions. She knew, without having experienced it before, that in this situation she was expected to accept Manus's behaviour totally, that she was not entitled to any explanation or any apology. All is fair in love and war. That is what people said. But even though she felt that it was stepping out of line she felt she would do it. Promising herself that gave her enough relief to go to sleep. In fact she had slept well.

Olaf looked dubious.

"Don't you think it's a good idea?"

"I suppose it could not do much harm. But I do not think it will do much good either."

"It would do me good to talk to him about it, I think. I think I should do that."

Sally's face was drawn under its tan and there were puffy paunches under her eyes from crying too much. She had brushed back her hair and tied it up with a ribbon – she had been wearing it down, under her handkerchief, as she worked in the fields – and she had put on a clean blouse and bodice. But she was not looking her best. She did not know that, however. She wasn't seeing herself, or anything else, very objectively at this moment.

She set off for the McLoughlins' shop. She had no very clear idea of how she would behave or what she would do once she got there. Manus was not visible in the shop as a rule, she remembered that, and it would take enormous courage for her to go to the back and knock on the door of the store, or march up to the counter and ask for him by name. She didn't think about it as she strode along the road, oblivious to all that surrounded her: men and women reaping and gathering in the fields of corn, the brambles laden with ripening fruit, the dog roses and honeysuckle that scented the air even in this early part of the day. She didn't even see the people that she met along the way. They looked after her and thought, "She's going somewhere in a hurry!" The truth was she was filled with a sense of purpose and with hope and for the first time in the two or three days since her conversation with Maura she felt, not happy, but not so desperately unhappy. She knew that as soon as she was with Manus everything would be all right. There would be some explanation that would clarify things and restore her to normality.

She reached the shop in record time. It seemed that she had hardly walked at all and yet there it was in front of her: a big whitewashed building, set slightly apart from the other houses in the village, with a red window and doorway, a red roof, piles of timber, sacks, coils of rope on the ground outside, boots and reaping hooks and scythes hanging from hooks outside the door, the window full of packets of tea. Someone had done a special display: boxes of Lipton's, Horniman's, Peoka, were all ranged in a fancy design.

She peeped in the door. He was not there. His father stood behind the counter in his brown coat, talking to some customer. He saw Sally come in, as he saw everyone: a bell rang as soon as anyone pushed open the door. But he did not acknowledge her and she left again hurriedly.

She walked around to the side of the building. She knew, from seeing people come in and out before, that the entrance to the store was there. And she was right. There was a door, red like the front door, with a sign on it saying "Private". She took a deep breath, counted to ten, and knocked on the door.

Nobody answered.

She knocked again, louder this time.

She heard footsteps inside. They approached the door. The latch was lifted inside, the door opened. Manus stood there. Manus, looking exactly as he had always looked, tall, broad-shouldered, curly-haired. His skin was slightly more golden than usual, after the holiday. That was the only change. Manus had answered the door. It was as easy as that, as easy as knocking on a door. Sally felt lucky.

"Manus!" she said. "Can I talk to you for a minute?"

His face turned cold. She had never seen such a closed, hard face.

"No," he said and shut the door.

"It was not such a good idea then?" Olaf was miserable. Sally was in a worse state than ever now.

"No." She couldn't talk about it any more.

"Sally. You are better off without him."

Sally said nothing at all. She did not cry any more either.

"He is not as grown up as he seems. He is not grown up enough for you. And he is cruel."

"He's always been very nice. He is a *nice* person." She leaped to his defence. It is not comforting to be told that you have been in love with someone who is no good.

"He is a merchant. It is his profession to be nice. All Irish people seem to have that profession anyway. You are all far too busy being nice to each other, and underneath maybe you are not so nice after all."

This was the kind of generalisation which aroused Sally's interest, in spite of how rotten she was feeling.

"What do you mean?"

"Oh, I do not know. I mean that in Iceland we are not so nice to each other all the time. Maybe we say what we mean. Maybe it is easier in the end?"

"You mean that what he has done is easier for me in the end?"

"What he has done is unforgivable. If you were a woman in an Icelandic saga you would ask your brother to go and kill him. And he would do that too! But you are not in an Icelandic saga."

"I wouldn't want to kill him anyway. I'd much rather kill myself."

"Ah, Sally! My Sally! It is healthier to be in a saga. But, Sally, there are a lot of boys in the world. You know that. Soon you will have forgotten all about him."

Sally smiled. She did not believe it for one second.

Troubles do not come singly, and that was not an end to Sally's.

She had neglected to visit Bridgie Greene for a few days, although Olaf had dutifully brought over the milk and administered doses of his medicine to Dónal, whom he reported was improving. It took Sally a week to feel capable of paying a call to anyone. In the meantime, she continued to help with the harvesting. There was no getting out of that, and the work helped her to hide her feelings if not, yet, to forget about them. When she finally called to the yellow hut, she found Bridgie in a bad way. She was sitting at her battered old table with her head in her hands.

"What is it, Bridgie? Is it Dónal?"

Dónal was lying on the bed in the corner, dressed in his white petticoat. His black ringlets were matted around his pale emaciated cheeks, and his big eyes were open.

He was dead.

18

Farewell

Dónal had died that day. The doctor, Eileen Carr's father, was called in by Sally and Miss Lynch when the child was already dead. He diagnosed leukaemia.

"Cancer of the blood," he explained. "Nothing could have been done for him anyway." There were tears in his eyes. It was not easy being a country doctor. "It would have been better if I had been called earlier, but I wouldn't have been able to save him. There is no cure. It is a case of gradual weakening. Poor little mite. He doesn't seem to have suffered pain, that's the only consolation."

"She is heartbroken," said Miss Lynch. Both she and Sally were at the hut trying to do what they could. The little girls were bewildered. Bridgie was going out of her mind with sorrow.

"I'll give her this sedative. It's nothing, just a little opiate. It will calm her down for the next few days and help her to get over it, God help the poor woman. If she had somewhere to live itself . . . Is there anyone to mind the children for her?"

"We'll mind them," said Sally quickly. "My mother, and I.

They know me quite well, we'll take them for a few days, if she wants it. She might not though."

"Who are you, miss?" asked the doctor, with a smile. He was a grey-haired man with a moustache and a beard. He looked like Parnell on the posters Sally used to see years ago.

"Sally Gallagher. A neighbour."

"Sally? Yes, I think I've heard of you before. You are a good girl, Sally. Take care of yourself."

"Thank you." His trivial but kind remarks and manners made Sally glow inside. Eileen Carr's father. He was a kind and a civilised man. She did not know why that should make her feel better, but it did. "Will you call back to see Bridgie?" she asked, looking him in the eye.

"I'll be back at the end of a week. The worst of it is usually when the funeral is over. I'll come again then. Good day to you now, Sally. Goodbye, Emily."

That was news to Sally. Miss Lynch's name: nobody in Glenbra School had ever known what it was.

As Sally guessed, Bridgie did not want the girls to leave the hut, and in the end Sally agreed that it was better that they stay with their mother. Having them to look after meant that she could not lose herself completely in her grief. Sally, however, prevailed upon her to let them come over to the house and play with Janey for a couple of hours every afternoon in the weeks that followed the funeral. This was good for the girls and good for their mother, who needed some time to be alone. It was also very good for Janey. She loved having some other children around the place and they had hilarious afternoons chasing around the farmyard, playing boats in the stream that ran behind the house, and a thousand and one other games.

The summer was drawing to a close. Already school was open: Janey was trotting up to the schoolhouse, usually on her own, every morning. The corn and oats had been thrashed and the sacks of grain were in the barn. Some had already been taken by Packy and Olaf to the mill and ground into meal. Sally loved to pick up a handful as she passed the sacks and let the dry, fresh meal run through her fingers. The early potatoes were mainly picked and stored in the covered pit for winter. The rest were ripening in the beds. The wool had all dyed, finally, and the hanks of russet, purple, red and black sent off by the agent to the mill. Soon, they hoped, lengths of tweed and plain cloth would be returned and the Gallaghers would all have fine new clothes. For the wedding.

It was to take place early in October. Katie would return a few weeks before the end of her term to be at it: her employers were decent people, and promised to let her go at no loss of pay. They were hoping that she would come back to them for the winter. Mrs Gallagher insisted that it would be a quiet affair, as was fitting for two older people like herself and Packy. But even so she planned on having a party, and had baked a fruit cake and prepared several hundred jars of jam, rhubarb, gooseberry, blackberry, and blackcurrant, with this partly in mind.

Olaf was still with them, still sleeping on the kitchen floor. He had exchanged his white clothes for a pair of homespun trousers and a tweed jacket that had once belonged to Jack, Sally's father. He was always very busy working on the farm, fixing things, fishing and hunting. There was hardly a night that the Gallaghers did not have roasted rabbit, or fresh salmon or trout, or some other delicacy that he had trapped or caught, for dinner. When he was not engaged in any of these activities, he was practising his acrobatics or else making something at the kitchen table: he could make dolls, all kinds of model animals, picture frames, from bits of driftwood which he found on the beach or bog oak that he picked up in the bog. The house was full of interesting ornaments and toys.

He had many conversations with Sally about life and love. Gradually she was getting over the break with Manus. It still hurt her, and it always would, but it hurt less and less as time went on. "Time is a great healer," her mother said, referring to Bridgie Greene's bereavement. Like many old sayings it had more than a grain of truth in it.

Olaf was a great healer, too. Having him around helped Sally more than anything else. He was someone she could confide in. He was cheerful and light-hearted. He was wise beyond his years – whatever they were. Sally never found that out; Olaf had some secrets from her.

"You are so busy," she said.

"That is the important thing in life," he said, "to keep busy. You should find things to do."

"I am usually busy," Sally was ruffled. "I'm no Lady Muck, sitting idly by."

"Yes, but perhaps you are not busy in the right way. You should find something that you really love to do, something that makes you completely happy. Then you will always be happy. Your happiness will be in yourself, not in somebody else."

"What is it you really love to do?"

"Many things. But mainly acrobatics. I think that is my favourite thing."

"I don't know what my favourite is. Reading, maybe. That used to be it."

"I do not see you reading much."

"No, I haven't had many books lately, somehow. I don't know why."

But she did. The reason was that she had been so busy with Manus all summer that she had hardly ever visited Miss Lynch, or tried to get any books.

"I must do something about that. Crocheting is out. I just do not like it."

She had tried out the crocheting class that Miss Lynch had told her about, but realised that such work was not for her. Her hands were too clumsy, she had no interest in the designs, she could not find the patience to complete the complicated patterns of flowers, birds, and leaves that they were required to do on the edges of handkerchiefs and table cloths.

"The winter is coming and I am going away soon. You should think of what you will do."

"You're going away?" Sally was dismayed. She had not given the matter any thought, but it had looked as if Olaf were going to stay on and on forever.

"My boat will be going back to Iceland and I want to be on it. I must see my family."

"Maybe your boat has gone already?"

"I don't think so. But there will be another boat if that is the case. There are boats coming from Reykjavik and the Faroes from time to time, to Killybegs and Sligo and some of the other ports. I am not worried about not being able to return."

"But will you come back? Will we see you again?" Sally was aghast at the idea.

"I may come back. I like it in Ireland, even though you are all a bit too nice. But next summer . . . I do not know. I want to travel around. I want to see other places. Next summer I might be in Scotland, or Norway, or the Faroe

146

Islands. I will do like I did here. Go from
play tricks. I have spent a long time with you
missed some fairs."

"Oh dear."

"Maybe you would like to come with me? Maybe y
would like to come to Iceland and to see the world?"

"Olaf! You mean to travel around with you, from fair to
fair, as you say?"

"Yes. Travel with me and see the world with me."

"I can't stand on my head. I can't even turn a
cartwheel."

"No. But you could dress up in a silk dress and put a
scarf around your hair and tell fortunes."

"Like Madame Rosa?"

"You'd be better than Madame Rosa. I know you
would."

Sally looked sadly at Olaf. He was so handsome, tall
and thin, with his shock of yellow hair, his open, smiling
face. He was, in a way, much more handsome than Manus.
And she felt so well when she was with him, light-hearted
and free. He still had that effect on her. He was a breath of
fresh air.

"I love you, Olaf," she said. "I really love you. But I am
not in love with you."

"No. You reserve that for bad-mannered men who will
treat you badly," he said, bitterly.

"That's not fair."

"You are right. It is not fair. And I know it is not true."

"No. It is not true."

"But then, Sally, if you do not want to see the world,
we will have to say goodbye. I will pack my bags and go,
tomorrow."

"You won't wait until Mother's wedding?"

"Oh no, I cannot wait for that. I must go as soon as possible, I want to be in Iceland before the winter sets in."

"Can I write to you? Can I be in touch with you?"

"Oh yes. I am not sure if I can read English and I know I can't write it. But perhaps I learn. You can write to me. Olafur Baldursson, Skari, Iceland. That is my address."

"That's all?"

"That's all."

19

New Directions

*K*atie came back. The Greene girls, Molly and Susie and their brother Tarry, returned from Scotland with twenty pounds saved between them. Mrs Gallagher and Packy Doherty got married.

"He's quite nice really when you get used to him," Sally whispered to Katie. They were standing in the church. It was a Sunday, the first Sunday in October. The fine weather had continued right into the autumn and a ray of gentle yellow light lay across the aisle.

Their mother and Packy walked up, linking arms.

Mrs Gallagher was dressed in a blue skirt and jacket, and she wore a blue hat with roses on the brim. Packy looked quite handsome in a dark brown suit. He had a rose in his buttonhole and had even removed his cap. Underneath he had a fine head of light grey hair.

"They look happy," said Katie. And they did. Especially Packy, who smiled broadly like the cat who has got the cream. Mrs Gallagher's expression was more reserved, but she seemed serene and content.

Katie had grown very tall over the summer and was looking beautiful herself. She wore a suit of the russet colour, made from the cloth they had dyed themselves, while Sally was in red. Janey sat between them, rigged up in a white dress, not sure whether she was happy or frightened. The other guests included all the Greenes, some of Packy's relations – he had a brother whom Katie couldn't stand – and a few others. Sally had, in a moment of forgiveness, sent a note via Janey to Maura McLoughlin inviting her to come along to the wedding. But she had not replied and was not in the church. Sally could have kicked herself for having made the gesture. But she thought of what Olaf would have said: "How could you know that she would respond in that way? You did the right thing."

Sally found herself often thinking of Olaf in just that way, wondering what he would think or say in a given situation, especially if it was a problematical one. He was, she realised, an unusually wise person. He was like a saint, really, or a hermit. And the more she thought of him the more she began to wonder if she had imagined everything about him. He had arrived like an angel or a ghost, tumbling along in his white clothes, like someone who had come down from the sky. He had stayed and worked and given good counsel, and then he had disappeared. The night he had told Sally he was leaving he had said goodbye to everyone, kissing them all, even Granny, and thanking them for their hospitality. The following morning when they got up he was gone.

The only thing that reminded Sally that he was not a ghost were all the wooden carvings that lay here and there around the house and that provided Janey with fascinating playthings for many a day to come.

The wedding ceremony was over. The family and

guests returned to the house where they had a breakfast of bacon, potatoes, apple pie. There was porter to drink and Donegal whiskey, distilled in Belfast, for the men. The big Greene boy played the accordion, and Elizabeth Gallagher, who was one of the guests, as well as Katie and Sally, sang songs. A quiet wedding, everyone said. But it was as happy as these occasions usually are. Mrs Gallagher became more and more radiant as the day wore on, and she realised that she had made the right choice: she liked being married again. Being the centre of attention at a wedding was not unappealing to the vain streak in her. More importantly, she liked Packy, with his quiet, kind ways, more and more as time went on. Packy was going to move into her house. He would continue to farm his own land, which was only two miles away. The house, which he half owned already, he would rent. That was the best part of it all as far as Sally was concerned. He would rent his old house to Bridgie Greene. She could move out of the yellow railway carriage and live in a proper house, paying a low rent for as long as it suited her. "I will pay the right rent if I can at all," Bridgie said, proudly. She was going to the crochet lessons, the oldest pupil in the school, and she had high hopes of her ability to earn money once she had learned how to do it properly. Besides, she had three children out earning already and two still to go, as she said herself, clinging sadly to the youngest girl.

It was during the wedding that Sally decided what she would do.

The thought came into her head, and she asked herself what Olaf would say. "That is a good idea," was what he would say, she thought. "And I think it is a good idea too," she answered. The day after the wedding she wrote a letter to Geraldina Bannister, the Visitor, and asked her to help her find a job in Dublin. She did not want to go to Iceland, or Scotland, or America, telling fortunes to strangers. But there was a part of the world she did want to see. She wanted to go to Dublin.

The reply came a week later. The Visitor was most enthusiastic. She gave Sally the train timetable, she begged her to write, she would meet her at the station. She had no fixed offers as yet, she had only received the letter and had had no time to make inquiries. But she knew there would not be the slightest difficulty. Everyone was looking for a nice Irish-speaking girl. Half of Dublin was trying to learn Irish. They were queuing up to get into classes at the Gaelic League, to go to Irish dancing classes, to play Gaelic football. Sally must come as soon as possible, she would have a field day. Everyone would be delighted to meet her since she was now a famous face in Dublin, the letter finished, "as the enclosed will illustrate!!!"

Enclosed with the letter, in a separate tissue envelope, were three glossy postcards. They showed Mrs Gallagher, sitting outside her own door, spinning. That card was labelled "The Donegal Spinning Wheel". The second card showed the farmyard and was labelled "Farmyard, County Donegal". And the third was Sally, with her shawl around her head, standing beside old Ned the ass. That was called "An Irish Colleen. Copyright Wm Lawrence, Sackville St".

"So you're copyright, Sally!" Katie joked. "What does that mean now I wonder?"

Everyone agreed that Sally looked lovely in the picture. Granny said it was the work of the devil and they should have had no part in it.

Two weeks later Sally was packing once more, preparing to set off on a new adventure in Dublin. She was in high spirits. Once she had made up her mind to do this, she knew it was the right decision.

The night before she was due to leave she was walking along the road, as she still did every evening. It was autumn now, and the evening was closing in already at seven o'clock. The boreen was littered with damp leaves. Sally pulled her shawl around her.

"Sally!"

She jumped.

"Sally, can I talk to you for a minute?"

Manus. He was standing under the oak tree where he had always met her. His face was tanned, after the summer, but he looked exhausted.

Sally stared at him. It occurred to her that she ought to turn on her heel and walk away. But she didn't move.

"I'm sorry," Manus said. "I'm really sorry."

"Oh," she shrugged. "Well . . . " She could think of nothing better to say.

"Will you walk along the road for a bit?"

"All right."

Manus smiled. He came closer to her and she could see that he was crying. They walked along together, awkwardly and silently, for a few minutes.

"How have you been keeping?"

"I've been fine," said Sally.

"Good. I've missed you terribly."

Sally felt a lump come to her throat.

"Have you?"

"Yes, I have."

"Well . . . I've missed you too."

Tears came to Sally's eyes. But she pushed them back.

"I'm sorry. I don't know why I did that."

"Don't you?"

"No. It was terrible. But I didn't know what else to do at the time. I'm sorry."

"Oh dear. I wish you'd stop saying you were sorry."

"Sorry."

They laughed.

"Listen. I will forgive you, if you stop saying you're sorry. All right?"

"I don't know how you can. I love you, Sally."

"I know. That's the reason."

They smiled together then. Sally felt both happy and sad at the same time.

After a while Manus said: "I hear you are going to Dublin."

"That's right."

"When are you going?" His voice became anxious.

"Tomorrow."

"Tomorrow? Oh, Sally, Sally!" He put his arm around her and kissed her cheek.

"I've got a job. I'm getting the train from Strabane on Tuesday."

"I wish you wouldn't go."

"I would have stayed, probably, if . . . "

"Couldn't you change your mind?"

Sally looked at him. She thought she had never seen a more beautiful human being, with his light hair and his brown skin, his dark serious eyes. He was so sad now, pleading with her, like a little child begging. He who had seemed so hard and relentless a few months earlier.

Her heart filled with love for him.

How easy it would be to stay.

"How long would it last?" Olaf's voice popped into her head. And there was Olaf, his yellow-haired head leaning quizzically to one side, his eyes laughing. "See the world,

Sally. Or for God's sake at least see Dublin. Do something for yourself. He will wait. People always wait if they love someone."

"I can't change my mind, Manus. Not now," she said slowly. Olaf receded from her, waving goodbye cheerfully. "I love you. And I forgive you; I think I understand why you behaved like that. But I can't change my mind."

"Oh Sally!" Manus started to cry openly. Sally comforted him, patting his head and caressing him, the way she comforted Janey when she fell and cut her knee.

"I'll be home for holidays," she said. "I'll probably be home for Christmas. And you can always come to visit me in Dublin, can't you?"

He nodded doubtfully.

"And we can write. Letters. We never did before but I'd like to do that now."

"I've never written any letters."

"Time to start," said Sally, cheering up herself at the prospect. "And now I have to go home. I've an early start tomorrow."

Arm in arm they walked back along the lane to Sally's house.

And the next morning, when the sun had just risen over the hills and the cock had crowed, Sally set off on the long journey south to Dublin.

Also by Poolbeg

The Hiring Fair

By

Elizabeth O'Hara

It is 1890 and Parnell is the uncrowned king of
Ireland. But thirteen-year-old Sally Gallagher,
"Scatterbrain Sally" as her mother and younger sister
Katie call her, has no interest in politics. She is happy
to read books and leave the running of the house to
those who like housework.

A shocking tragedy changes the lives of the sisters.
Instead of being the daughters of a comfortable
Donegal farmer and fisherman, they have to become
hired servants, bound for six months to masters they
don't know.

Elizabeth O'Hara has written an exciting story that has
its share of sorrow and joy. She creates in Scatterbrain
Sally a new and unforgettable Irish heroine.